Large Mammals, Stick Insects & Other Social Misfits

About the author

A BBC staff journalist for twenty years during the Northern Ireland conflict, Felicity McCall began the millennium as a full-time writer as well as an occasional broadcaster, arts facilitator and actor. This is her fourteenth publication. Previous titles include fiction, non-fiction, plays and a graphic novel, and she has contributed to a number of anthologies.

The co-founder and director of two theatre companies, she has had twelve plays staged professionally and four screenplay credits. Felicity has won the Tyrone Guthrie Award for stage and screenplay and was nominated for two Meyer Whitworth Awards and two Irish Playwrights' and Screenwriters' Guild Awards for best new play. Felicity is the Ireland officer for the miscarriage of justice lobby group Portia, and she continues to live and write in Derry and Donegal.

Large M@mmals Stick Insects & other Social Misfits

FELICITY McCALL

Little Island

LARGE MAMMALS, STICK INSECTS & OTHER SOCIAL MISFITS
Published 2012
by Little Island
7 Kenilworth Park
Dublin 6W
Ireland

www.littleisland.ie

ISBN 978-1-908195-18-0

British Library Cataloguing Data. A CIP catalogue record for this book is available from the British Library.

Design by Someday

Printed in Poland by Drukarnia Skleniarz

Supported by **The National Lottery**® through the Arts Council of Northern Ireland

Little Island received financial assistance from
The Arts Council (An Chomhairle Ealaíon), Dublin, Ireland.

10 9 8 7 6 5 4 3 2 1

For the tweens and teenagers of the noughties who shared their life and light, became extended family and made our house a home. Especially Aine, Caoimhe, Christopher, Stacey and Trevor.

Acknowledgements

My thanks and appreciation to Elaina O'Neill, Siobhan Parkinson and all at Little Island for inspirational professional guidance, cheery encouragement and impeccable standards. And for believing in Aimée in the first place.

The Arts Council of Northern Ireland and its Literature Officer Damien Smyth for support and inspiration.

My fellow writers, theatre practitioners and artist/activists whose constructive criticism, cynical good humour and boundless energy never fail to sustain me through the writing process.

All my loved ones, for your generosity of spirit and faith ... you know who you are; I know how special you make my life.

And central among you, Aoife, always.

Chapter
One

I t all started when Mizz Hardy, the five foot two inches and 120 pounds of pure blonde sunshine (I don't think) that constituted 12G's form teacher asked, nay, commanded us to produce a personal profile. I remember the time exactly. It was the Friday afternoon of the first full week of the new school year. September the ninth, second period after lunch. Just after Steven McQuillan got a break time for sending Carly Jenkins a note which, when opened, was found to contain nine dead wasps. Carly screamed so much she was sent outside the room to compose herself.

'What do we put in the profile Miss – Mizz?' That was Barry Bradley, class cretin, always first in with the obvious question. I think it's a reassurance thing with him. A sort of comfort ritual.

'Everything and anything. Make it vibrant!' trilled Mizz, who has never given any pupil a straight answer in her life. 'Vibrant and electric!' she enthused, waving her multi-coloured charity wristbands. This got the inevitable snigger from Barry's sidekick Sleazeball, aka Simon Costas-Kelly.

When there was no reaction to his snigger, Sleaze leaned across and banged my co-best friend, Rebekah O'Hara, hard in the ribs.

'I thought she was going to say vibra–'

'We know what you thought, you idiot,' hissed Rebekah, and Mizz, catching the sound if not the content of their exchange, glared down at her.

'As I said, class, make it fresh and dynamic. Inviting. Vibrant!' That was obviously the buzzword of the day. 'Make your paired pupil want to get to know you.'

Paired pupil? Time to stop daydreaming about next week's Firewall disco – eight days to go and counting – and concentrate on the subject in hand.

I vaguely took in the information that a dozen or so of us had been selected to take part, pending parental consent, in a twinning scheme with a school in south Dublin. Foxrock, to be precise. Dublin 18. Mizz had quoted Wikipedia: 'A leafy garden suburb of some eleven thousand citizens.' This school, Knockgorey, operates something like our Purpose-built Integrated Castle Grove College here in Derry. It prides itself on welcoming those of all faiths or none. All-ability, naturally. Knockgorey was de facto integrated, Mizz said, without explaining further, except to say it joined us in leading the way in breaking down boundaries in education.

That's the theory, anyway. I don't know about Knockgorey but, in practice, Castle Grove is more of a home from home/dumping ground for the idealists, the conscientious objectors, the politically correct, the don't-knows, the floating voters, the immigrant workers, the American diaspora and the offspring of what are hilariously referred to as 'mixed marriages'. (Is there any other kind? I suppose there is, these days, now I come to think of it.)

I've been there since I was eleven and I love it to bits. So do my two best friends since day one in 8G, Rebekah O'Hara and Bree Harley.

Bree, I must add, was, by being in the lower – sorry, alternative – English group, already excluded from the twinning and would have to be consulted later about this development. She is not dense. Far from it. She's just a bit dreamy. And abstract. Especially when she thinks she's met The One. But I digress.

'Can we use photos?' This from Patricia Mooney, aka Wannabe, who fondly imagines herself to be a lookalike for a younger Megan Fox. In her dreams.

'You won't need to, Patricia. Those of you taking part in the scheme will eventually be in contact by webcam, anyway. In time, we hope to meet up at least once or twice. And for reasons of personal security and emotional well-being, you will be actively discouraged from making contact on social networking sites.' (By which she means Facebook. Just so you know.)

'Far better' – Mizz was just getting started – 'to create a profile that is a pot pourri of your favourite sounds, scents, star signs and seasons,' she alliterated. 'Your aspirations, hopes and dreams ...' Mercifully, the bell went, cutting her short before she burst into song.

We threw our books, pencil cases, make-up, warm bottled water and MP3 players into the life support systems laughably referred to as our school bags, and Rebekah and I idled our way out the door – we don't rush to technology, ever; it's a girl thing. Mizz was handing out letters addressed to our parents or guardians. Each student, it seemed, needed parental consent to take part in the scheme.

We met up with Bree at the end of the school day and walked to the bus stop together. While Rebekah updated Bree on the whole twinning scheme, I was mentally setting up my personal profile.

I am Aimée Logan. I'm a Sagittarian whose fave season is winter; fave scent is Clio's fresh morning coffee or Davidoff Cool Water, depending on the context; and fave sound is the welcome-home reassuring purring of my multi-striped cat – Rainbow by name (after the refuge where he adopted me), random by nature. The only child (me, I mean, not Rainbow) of journalist and local-activist-turned-social-reformer Eamonn Logan of 149 Beech Avenue and his ex-wife, the academic and lecturer Clio McCourt of 1A (A for ground floor) Riverview, aka the New Apartments. Aka flats. Clio – whom I aggravate by calling Mammy – and Eamonn – who is happy enough to be called Da except when he's in the company of Fiona's friends and is being economical about his age – split up when I was four and now live in happy separation as coparents and intellectual best friends. The aforementioned Fiona is my dad's present partner. Whatever.

In her youth, the Mammy had the distinction of being the only teenager ever to get herself arrested at a peace demonstration in the city. The Da was the trainee reporter sent to interview Clio and get a glammy pic at the same time. They spent all evening discussing the ethics of using force as the means to an end and the rest – aka me – is history. But now – oh, well, I'm fortunate to live in two generally conflict-free, non-judgemental zones, as I am free to come and go between the two. Mostly Riverview cause (1) it's tidier, (2) it has a more consistent standard of healthy cooking, (3) nearly all my clothes are there and (4) so is Rainbow.

As we arrived at the bus stop, Rebekah and I were si-multaneously thumbnailing open the twinning letters. But I already knew the phrases 'parental consent' and 'poor Rebekah' were inseparable. It's not that Rebekah's parents don't care; it's just that there were, at the last count, six and seven-ninths little O'Haras, three part-time jobs, a dependent granny, three benefit books and a peripatetic ex-combatant uncle (whom they get for the summer season which de facto extends to November before he comes back for The Christmas). So anything that involves extra expense, time or form-filling is out of the question. Rebekah probably wouldn't even tell them about the twinning until she'd turned it down.

She's amazing, Rebekah. She may be the eldest in an ever-extending line of progeny, but she never feels hard done by and she loves the little ones to bits. Only very oc-casionally, when stressed, does she threaten to make her mum read our sex – sorry, life-studies leaflets. Maybe that's why she, unlike Bree, hasn't even had an inkling about where she might find The One. She's not looking. She wouldn't have to. She's gorgeous: petite and dark with huge brown eyes, a heart- shaped face, perfect skin and an Irish tenor voice. The bitch.

'We could manage it between us ...' I made an attempt at persuading her.

She shook her head. 'There's always hassle about whose turn it is to use the PC in our house and you couldn't depend on using the computers in the school library ...'

'Parental consent's easy for me,' I said. 'This sounds like the sort of thing they'd be up for. Making friends and widening horizons, all that stuff.'

'You'll get twinned straight away,' Bree assured me. Bree Harley. Co-best friend, supermodel skinny, long red – sorry, strawberry blonde hair, snooker-room pallor (when you see her without her make-up, which isn't often).

'It's logical,' she went on. 'Think about it.' She consulted my letter. 'They want ten and two reserves – that's twelve' (she's OK at maths, even if she does insist that I do all her coursework for her) 'and there's about twenty in your English group ...'

'Eighteen.'

'Even easier, then. Say three or four can't manage it because of family stuff, like Rebekah. Then there's the weirds, like Simon, that are too risky to twin with anyone, even by Castle Grove standards. You'll get paired up no problem, even if your profile's self-obsessed shite – which it won't be,' she added quickly. 'We'll come round to the flat later and help you. Paul!

Paul! Hang on, wait a minute! Aimée, take my bag, pet, gotta go!'

And she ran off in a perfect diagonal which was the shortest distance between two points: (a) us, her best mates, and (b) Paul Kennelly, The One, who was loping out onto the edge of the asphalt track where the cross-country training was getting underway, all lanky legs and billowing PE kit.

'She cannot seriously be considering joining in?' I asked Rebekah as we got on the bus, watching our confused companion strip off her blazer and tie and join the line-up. 'She's wearing stilettos.'

'I reckon she just wants to show she's willing. You know, that she's up for sharing his interests. She doesn't actually have to run. Well, not far, anyway. She just has to double back to the line and wait for him to finish.'

'That could be hours.'

Rebekah reached up and patted me on the shoulder. 'It will indeed, Aimée, but you and I have never been In Love. Not even once.'

Sad, but true.

'You can't blame us. I mean, look around you.' I gestured. 'What do you see?'

'I know.' She nodded in agreement.

But I'd lost interest. 'Where's this Foxrock place, did she say?' I asked. I'm hazy on geography.

'It's south Dublin and really upmarket. Professional commuter-land.' Rebekah knows everything. 'You'll be able to do some networking, Aimée. Setting up contacts for when we go to Dublin, to university. In due course.'

Rebekah is alone in my peer group in that (a) she has a Life Plan, (b) she has researched it and (c) she will very

probably fulfil it. There's not much room for spontaneity or randomness in her life. She's going to be a child
psychologist. She's done the practical course already.

'And as for Bree,' she went on, 'new faces and plenty
of them are just what she needs.'

'You don't think that Paul is The One, then?'

Rebekah laughed. 'I suppose he has the advantage
of being younger than her mother's boyfriends. That's
something.'

Mammy Bree, I should explain here – currently aka
Sorcha, baptismal name Sarah – 'found herself' on a
mixed-discipline arts foundation course some six years ago
and has been working feverishly on preserving the rein-
vention ever since. She spends her days – and a good
many nights – at a community arts outreach centre
peopled by cute denim-clad men in their early twenties,
not all of whom are gay. She is ubiquitous without anyone
being sure what exactly she does or if she gets paid for it.
Daddy Bree, a son of the soil reassuringly answering to
Willie, returned to his roots when he and Sorcha parted
and now tills the soil somewhere in Donegal.

There is an ultra-desirable older sister too, Sinéad –
current ID uncertain, possibly Storm – who is said by
her mother to be 'exploring creativity through the
medium of dance in greater London'. Aka pole dancing
in an Irish pub in Kilburn.

'Aimée! This is our stop! What's up with you anyway?'

Rebekah tucked the consent letter back in my blazer
pocket, with a big felt-pen asterisk on it to remind me to
get it signed. Maybe new horizons were indeed opening
up. If that's what horizons do.

Chapter Two

ebekah and I parted to go in opposite directions at our bus stop. I plodded up to my front door in a manner akin to a beast of burden, with my rucksack slung over one shoulder and Bree's – which is, unbelievably, even heavier – over the other, slightly unbalancing me. The door opened to a six-legged welcome: the Mammy, clutching her omnipresent notepad, and Rainbow, chasing Clio's pen across the hall floor.

'Remind me to write to the school again about getting lockers for you. It's ridiculous you girls carrying that weight on your back every day. Once you get a weak back, it's with you for life.'

Well, obviously. Like, where would it go? But that's the Mammy – one sniff of a cause or an injustice and she's away. Impassioned.

'Childbirth is hard enough on your spine. I thought the parents' committee was taking it up with the school. I must get on to them again. How are you, love? Good day?'

'All right,' I said. 'Not much craic. Carly Jenkins got put out of class for screaming about dead wasps. I'm starving. Is there any smoky cheese? Oh, and can you sign this?'

I handed her the consent form. She always reads them before signing them, which is laudable but a pain.

'Is Bree still all loved up?' she asked while she was reading, marking the spelling and typographical errors as she went for future evidence of declining teaching standards to produce at the next governors' meeting. (I didn't mention that before as it's embarrassing at times – she's a parent governor.)

'Yeah,' I replied between mouthfuls of sandwich. I never know why she's fascinated with Bree's alleged love life. Perhaps because neither she nor I – that I know of – has one. Or because she sees it as the subject for a lecture, even a seminar. Possibly a short conference.

'She hasn't an ounce of wit. She's fifteen, Aimée, for God's sake ...'

I knew to interrupt this mid-flow before it became a forty-minute diatribe on women who love too much, the nature of infatuation or some similar theme, which she never fails to warm to. My granny says Clio was injected with a gramophone needle and, once she explained to me what that is, I had to agree.

'This twinning with Knockgorey College sounds interesting,' I mumbled as sincerely as I could, and the lecture switched to a tried and tested one on integration, cross border co-operation, mutual understanding etc., etc., etc. As I nodded and chewed, the phone and doorbell rang simultaneously. The Mammy got the phone first.

'Cliona speaking.'

Cliona. Dear God. This sounded serious. Nobody, not even Granny, calls her Cliona. Ever. Most of my friends think her proper name's Cleopatra.

Persistent ringing at the door ruled out the possibility of further eavesdropping. It was Bree, clearly upset and equipped with a pout, calling to collect her school bag, raid the fridge for munchies and my wardrobe for possible outfits for the Firewall and seek the Mammy's worldly wisdom for advice on Paul.

Bree can project tragic abandon on a grand scale. It's a gift. Even Rainbow, no stranger to emotional blackmail himself, falls for it every time and embeds himself, purring empathetically, in her lap.

Half an hour later, the entire contents of my (limited) wardrobe were strewn over the bedroom and the hand-wash-only items smeared with fake tan gel. The remains of a can of sparkling E-numbers were soaking into the faux sheepskin rug and Bree had decamped to the kitchen and was perched on a stool at the breakfast bar, legs outstretched at right angles until the tanning gel soaked in. At least she spread sheets of paper from the recycling pile under her thighs to protect the woodwork, in case she momentarily forgot her muscle-tone and her legs collapsed.

'Is this the male psyche thing, Clio, d'you think?' she asked disingenuously, all limpid eyes and puzzled pout. 'You know, like men are from Venus and women are from Mars and all that.'

I threw my eyes up but didn't bother to put her right. She'd forget anyway.

'Tell me it all again, only more slowly, love,' the Mammy said as she multitasked, stirring pasta sauce, setting out plates and cutlery, tickling Rainbow's tum with her big toe and probably rehearsing tonight's women's group agenda in her head. Which is why she missed the finer points the first time.

'Well,' Bree began again, 'it started when I just sort of strolled over, casually like' – yeah, about as casually as a greyhound out of a trap – 'to watch the start of the cross-country training and I caught a glimpse of Paul in the line-up. I just wanted to show I'm willing to share in his interests – bonding, if you like.' (What a cheese she is!) 'And he seemed sort of … embarrassed, like he didn't want to see me.'

'Maybe he *was* embarrassed.' Clio's tone was soothing. 'Adolescent males sometimes find it difficult to handle open physical shows of affection, especially if their parents haven't brought them up in a demonstrative environment …'

Oh my God, she was off again. I was saved by the phone – another 'Cliona speaking' job – and hustled the sticky-limbed one back into the bedroom to make her watch me tidy it.

'What was with all that?' I demanded once the door was shut.

'Don't be so hard on your mum, Aimée. She makes me feel … valued. I like that, y'know.'

More buzzwords. I was sorting garments into piles of handwash, coloureds and whites.

'So what really happened next?' I asked. 'Why did you tear off after him?'

Bree had the grace to look shamefaced. 'I wanted to find out if he really was training, like he said.'

'What else would he be doing at four o'clock on a Friday afternoon dressed in super-sized PE gear and ancient trainers?'

'It's just … well … you'll think I'm silly.'

'Probably, but go ahead.'

'Patricia said she heard from her sister's boyfriend that Paul's ex-girlfriend wants back with him and –'

'And what? And you believed her?'

'Well, he is fit.'

A dramatic pause from me, weighted with implications.

'He *is*,' insisted the loved-up one.

'Yeah. Right.'

'Don't be so jealous, Aimée. Just cause …'

Cause what? Cause I think he looks like a stick insect in a shroud? Cause I think she is so sad at times? Cause I don't have a crush myself right now? Cause I don't have the courage to admit to it when I do and risk public humiliation? Cause who on God's earth would look at a beast with an attitude problem like me when there are totally fanciable, readily available people like Bree walking this earth?

'So, did you follow him?'

'At that speed? These are Sorcha's stilettos, Aimée. I'd have wrecked the heels. Do you think I'm tired of living?

No,' she went on sadly, 'I waited round for ages, like, fifteen minutes, then I got fed up and hungry and I remembered my make-up was in my school bag and it was on the bus with you so I came here.'

'Bree,' I said reasonably, 'it's an hour and a half run.'

'Well, then,' she concluded brightly, 'I'm better off here. I can stalk him later. Don't be grumpy,' she added, cajoling. 'You're my bestest friends, you and Rebekah, and I want to get you two all glammed up for the Firewall. Now, if I'm wearing your green top, which I am, cause Paul says I look cute in green, even though it is a bit big on me, and Rebekah is borrowing your new denim mini, cause she's got great legs – short but great – not that it doesn't suit you,' she went on hurriedly, 'I can put a couple of darts in it for her ... Well, what are you wearing?'

'Whatever's left in my wardrobe that's clean? If there is anything.'

'You're being grumpy again, Aimée. I'll do your make-up, OK? And if you can only think who you want to get off with, I can work on setting you up. We'll do a list. You like lists, don't you? Like your mum?'

Dear God, is that how I am seen by the rest of 12G? The Classmate Who Likes Lists?

'Is there no one you fancy – even a bit?'

Bree's tone was persuasive.

'No. Not really.'

'Not REALLY? So there is someone. A bit?'

'No.'

'C'mon, Aimée, you're too ... fussy. Selective. Picky. What about Mickey Martin?'

'No way. Infectious.'

'Gareth?'

'A wanker.'

'OK, Simon? He likes you.'

'Bree. Go away, *now*, if you want to live.'

'Just for the hands-on experience, Aimée. I could put a word in for you –'

'No. N-O. Experience of what? Sweaty palms and halitosis?'

'OK. OK. Let's go for casual but smart. Rebekah!'

Rebekah had arrived into the room, accompanied by the Mammy and a bundle of newspapers.

'Rebekah's come to help you with your personal profile,' said Clio. 'I think that's a great idea, Rebekah, bringing the local papers. You could scan some of the main articles, to give your twin pal an idea of everyday life here,' she enthused.

'Youth Aggro Causes City Centre Chaos' read one headline. 'Stop this Teenage Drinking Culture' was another. They probably came straight from the laptop of the Da. Just the impression Castle Grove's governors would want to give our southern counterparts. I don't think.

'Want anything to drink? Anything to eat?'

The Mammy is hospitable in the extreme, I'll give her that. Having only produced me, I think she enjoys the company.

'No thanks, Clio, we'll get stuck into the computer first.'

This was unlike Rebekah. But we had a busy agenda, as she reminded us once the door closed behind the Mammy.

Here Rebekah brought out her list. (God, it must be true. Did I really ask her for a list?) 'It's simple,' she said. 'Double-check not babysitting. Treble-check Mammy for signs of premature labour. Borrow Aimée's denim mini – and can I have –'

'Take the yellow dolly shoes and vest as well,' I heard myself say. 'They do suit you better. Honestly. That vest is a bit stretched on me.'

'Thanks, Aimée, thanks.'

'Anyway,' I said, 'I'm doing smart but casual. Bree's reinventing me.'

'You should embrace your curves,' Beks suggests. 'Think Kelly Brooke. Think Bootylicious.'

Think Spanx pants.

Beks takes my silence for the dismissal it is.

'The black trousers again then?' she says.

'Probably.'

'Where are they? I don't see them,' interrupted Bree.

'I have to roll sticky tape over them a few more times to get rid of the last of the cat hairs.'

'OK.'

'I haven't got a list,' said Bree. 'Except, "snog Paul".'

'Bree,' said Rebekah, all big-sisterly concern, 'are you sure he's The One? I mean –'

'Rebekah. Sensible is worse than sarcastic. Chill. OK?'

'OK, OK,' said Rebekah. 'Now, let's get going on the profile. I may not be putting my name forward' – Bree and I glanced at each other – 'but it's all right, really it is. The time's not right. And remember, we want Aimée to be twinned with someone who …'

'Who has amazing friends,' Bree cut in, 'and whose parents are loaded. Then whoever it is can invite us to stay at her place and meet her older brothers who are all sex gods – for you two, of course,' Bree added hastily. 'I'm spoken for.' Then she stood up and said, 'I'll charm Clio into making us vitamin-enriched smoothies and you two can start typing. Give us those papers, Rebekah; we might get some ideas from the personal ads ... y'know, "Lonely teenager, metabolically challenged, seeks soulmate".'

Metabolically challenged! Worthy of Clio, that. I think I'd rather she just came out with it straight: fat. By her thinspirational standards, if not by the medical charts.

'Sometimes ...' I began and Rebekah nodded.

'I know. She doesn't mean any harm, really. So, let's start with the basics. How about something like this? "Irish cinema, Taco sauce, Donegal beaches at sunset, boho style and cats – these I like. Bigotry, racism, the Atkins diet, boy bands and disaster movies are so not me."'

'Whatever.'

'Or something controversial to attract attention? I dunno, maybe "Twin with me or you'll regret it!"'

'Hmm.'

Rebekah stared at me. 'What is it, Aimée? C'mon. Before Bree comes back and tries to cheer you up.' She stood up and gave me a hug.

I shrugged. 'Hormones.'

Truth was, maybe a soulmate was exactly what I was looking for. Assuming I had a soul. And that they mate.

'Speaking of hormones ...' Rebekah looked at me levelly, gauging my reaction, 'Mammy said she saw Fiona at the clinic today.' Pause. 'The antenatal. Today. Your da's Fiona.'

Oh. My. God.

'What was she doing?' (Idiot question, I know. Put it down to post-traumatic shock.)

'She was just there. Mammy nodded at her because they'd met somewhere before, but she didn't think Fiona recognised her.'

'There must be an explanation,' I said quickly. 'She was probably with a friend or something. She's not pregnant. I mean, I'm certain she's not. Not seven months anyway. The Da would have said. Even *he* couldn't fail to notice that.'

'I just thought I'd mention it.'

'Yeah.'

'In case someone else did.'

'Yeah.'

'She was probably with a girlfriend. A lot of the expectant mothers would be about her age. Thirtyish. And some of them come with the friend who's going to be their birthing partner. It's not just my dad who's terrified of the very thought of blood.'

'Yeah.'

'There are loads of teenagers, too. Mammy says sometimes she feels like a granny and she's only thirty-seven.'

'Yeah.'

'So I just thought I'd better mention it, you know? I mean, this city is a village.'

'Yeah. Thanks, Rebekah.'

But I was still thinking, Oh. My. God. Does the Mammy have any inkling? I'm sure she told me they – I mean he – had a vasectomy before they split up. There had to be a rational explanation. Didn't there?

'It's none of your bloody business, really,' commented Bree as she came back in, clutching a smoothie. She'd obviously been listening at the door. She does that.

'But calm your hormones, Aimée,' she added cheerfully, 'we'll investigate. Trust me.'

Chapter Three

Saturday. A day of rest. But not so in 1A Riverview Apartments. It was a day that did not dawn well. In fact, that particular Saturday showed every promise of being ill-starred, a non-event, or just plain shite.

Usually, I'm woken by a soft *pad-pad* across my bedroom floor, followed by the thump, wriggle and warm, furry suffocation of Rainbow taking up his habitual place curled round my head. That morning, it was the shrieks of an avenging angel – aka the Mammy – screeching his name, followed by a mouthful of unladylike expletives, uncomplimentary adjectives and threats of various forms of sensory deprivation that woke me. It appeared that the multi-striped one had been on the prowl for his favourite plaything – one of the

Mammy's gel pens – to Beckham about the floor with. But he had chanced upon the cylindrical plastic barrel containing the Mammy's contact lenses in their once-a-week deep cleansing solution and taken a free kick with it.

Result: total maternal panic. The lens case was now hidden from human view in some feline goalmouth, she knew not where, and Rainbow was giving no clues. Blind and agitated, her chances of finding it were nil unless I got up and helped. Without her lenses, the Mammy's field of vision isn't even a small lawn.

Our floor-level game of hide-and-seek was punctuated with phone calls to and from a 'Brian' (who?) to alter agendas and reschedule lifts and collection points (he's obviously work-related). I eventually found the thing wedged underneath the washing machine, coated with a goodly layer of dust and fluff.

After the daily miracle of sight restored, Brian was telephoned and ordered to revert to plan A. Then there was just time for a frenzied make-up session and a blast of quick-fire instructions aimed at me before the doorbell summoned her. It didn't seem a good time to ask her the morning's two most pertinent questions – whether the Da had had a vasectomy and who was on the phone last night – twice – when she identified herself as Cliona? Could it have been the aforementioned Brian?

'Did you get the profile finished?' she called over her shoulder, indicating the completed consent form on top of a list of handwritten instructions, a £10 note and a microwave box on a plate beside the phone, all of which told me she was out for the day. I'm sure she'd told me where, many times, but I had absolutely no recall.

'Not quite. I'll finish it this afternoon,' I lied as
Rainbow emerged from under the sofa and pounced on
the breakfast bar to lap up Clio's leftover muesli.

'I thought you and the girls were going up the town?
No? Bye, love, must go.' And she did.

It had been suggested among us girls, at one stage,
and in the absence of anything better to do, that we
should spend the afternoon searching for a new outfit for
me for the Firewall, but I couldn't raise any enthusiasm.
What was the point? Whatever we picked would end up
on Bree, who would look so gorgeous that when I DID
get my turn to wear my own new clothes, I'd look in the
mirror and think how much fatter and uglier I looked in
the same outfit. Then I'd chuck it into the back of the
wardrobe in disgust. I'd ignore it for a couple of weeks
and then end up giving it to her.

From past experience, the Firewall fashion show made
me realise what I was: overweight, if not medically obese.
Well, not really ... Curvelicious? Me? No. Chubby is the
proper term for it. With a round face, periodic outbreaks
of pus, hair which defies straightening and just – well, not
pretty. Nor sexy. Not striking. Not even so ugly as to
attract sympathy. Sure, I was seen as lively and organised
and clever, but what almost-sixteen-year-old wants to be
defined like that? Last night, every single item I'd tried on
– barring my PJs, and you can't go to the Firewall in them
– had felt tight and made me look bloated and bulging.

'Mid-cycle retention,' the Mammy assured me.
'Drink your eight glasses of water a day, avoid wheat and
processed foods, take your evening primrose oil and it'll
settle in a day or two.'

Oh, yes? Well, *chez* Bree they only drink water if there's a three-finger vodka in it to take away the taste, and their microwave is their life-support system. Yet they are all tall, lithe and lovely. And spot-free.

As for me being 'widely read and a competent debater', as my last term report said, well, those qualities don't help at a place like the Firewall. Whereas one look at Bree in her faded jeans with a little crop top emphasising her washboard stomach and young males no longer think with their brains.

No, hitting the shops would only compound my depression. Besides, Rebekah wanted to build up brownie points for the Firewall by taking a handful of small siblings for the afternoon, and Bree was involved in some fledgling and ill-fated scheme to set up a cross-country cheerleaders' group. It was best to sit down with Rainbow, my muesli and my faithful notepad and draw up a list.

Even in my morning torpor I washed out the cereal bowl Rainbow had been slurping from before refilling it and pouring myself a pint of juice. I tried it on the muesli but it was disgusting, honestly it was, so I opted for going minimal dairy (one portion) instead of dairy-free and started all over again with fresh muesli and milk, which is how God intended muesli to be eaten. Now – concentrate.

1

Vasectomy? How to approach subject tactfully?

2

If answer to (1) is yes, explanation for Fiona's presence at antenatal or, if not Fiona, investigate possibility that Mrs O'H is having a hallucinatory pregnancy or, worse, consuming dodgy mushrooms. Knowingly or not.

3

Who Brian? Why Brian?

4

If cheerleaders are to become a reality, I will have to get involved. Is it worth the grief?

5

Where is the Mammy, when will she be home and what is the £10 for?

At least some of these questions were resolved when I consulted the note Clio had left by the phone, which revealed that she was speaking at a one-day conference on 'The Gender Agenda'. Brian, 'an old colleague' (how old?), is also speaking; he is giving her a lift (mercifully she gave up her licence when she realised she couldn't really see the car in front of her, never mind read its number plate) and she is feeding him in return. (Where? When? How? It is unlike her to leave questions unanswered.) The £10 is towards the sports bra I told her I needed urgently to stop me knocking myself out in PE, and I am to try a D as well as a C cup before buying.

'P.S. DO try it on!!! Love Mammy/Clio.'

Feckfeckfeck. Up the town after all. And Mammy/Clio knows if there's one thing I hate, loathe and detest in the town, it's trying on bras.

I grabbed the phone, on to items (1) to (3) inclusive.

'Dad? Hi.'

'Hello?'

'It's Aimée.'

Who else is likely to be calling him Dad? Oh my God.

'I'll just switch off the radio; I can't hear you.'

Radio 1 at forty-something. That is so gross. He says he likes the tunes. *Tunes!*

'There we go. What are you doing, love?'

'Nothing much. Eating my breakfast.'

'Same here. Fiona's just cooked up a big fry – sausages, bacon, pudding, potato bread, the works.'

Not pregnant, then.

'Good of her when all she ever has is her hot water and lemon, first thing. Can't face solid food.'

Pregnant?

'Where's your mammy, anyway?'

'At a conference all day.'

'Oh, that's right, she mentioned that. We did something on it last Friday. The Gender Agenda. Good title. I suppose she thought of it. Brian O'Donnell's one of the keynote speakers. It was quite a coup getting him to Derry for a year.'

Brian the lift?

'D'you know him, Da?'

'Only to speak to. Your mammy knows him better than I do.'

How well?

'He's attached to her department while he's writing his PhD thesis.'

Aha. Fledgling Doctor Brian?

'What age is he, Da?'

'How do I know? I suppose he's, oh, maybe twenty-eight, twenty-nine, maybe a bit more – why?'

Dear Jesus, what is it with divorced parents? A cradle-snatching contest?

'Clio only mentioned it to me because she thought you might be glad of a bit of company. So we could pick you up later. But she said to check with you first in case you and the girls were going up the town.'

'Actually,' I ventured cleverly, 'we aren't this week. Bree's preoccupied with rosettes and ra-ra skirts and Rebekah's doing some extra babysitting. Mrs O'Hara's expecting again, you know. At the start of November. But she could go early, Beks says.'

'Is she? How many's that? Six? Seven? Has she heard about the population explosion?'

Good. My move. I attempted a nonchalant rhetorical question.

'Has she heard about contraception?' God, I can be so manipulative. Maybe I should be a barrister, not a life coach. 'They're a lovely family, though. They're very close,' I add. 'And I don't mean just in age.'

'One or two's enough, don't you think, Aimée?'

One or two? What about one?

'It's a wonder Mr O'Hara doesn't consider a vasectomy, or maybe he thinks it's too final.'

'Aimée! I know you're all for openness and accountability, but it really is none of your business. Maybe it's Rebekah's business, as she seems to half-rear them, but definitely not yours. Anyway, it can be reversible.'

Oh no. The random variable.

'What?'

'I said it can be reversible. Depends on the technique. Anyway, that sort of thing's no concern of yours – yet.'

I wish.

'So, never mind the O'Haras, what are you doing with yourself?' the Da continued. 'Fiona's going up the town later on. She wants to get some new girly things, as she calls them, so I'm supernumerary. I'm going for a pint and to watch the match while she's shopping. And then she's joining me when she's finished. D'you want our taxi to pick you up?'

Normally, no way. But – new girly things? Burgeoning boobs on the size 8 stick insect? Anti-stretch-mark cream? A chance for sharing feminine intimacies? A free taxi ride? (It was raining.)

'OK, that sounds good. What time?'

'I'm ordering the taxi for half past two. Make sure you're ready.'

'Right. See you then. Rainbow was playing football with Mammy's lenses this morning,' I added. I was just trying to keep him involved in the daily trivia of 1A Riverview. 'It could have been a tragedy.'

'That's nothing. I drank a pair once. They were in a glass of water she'd left beside the bed and I thought it was for me when I woke up with a hangover. Very thoughtful, you know. Her, not me. I wanted to check later in case they passed –'

'Da! Half two then! Bye!'

Does the male sense of humour really never leave the lavatory?

I decided to try Granny and enquire about her knowledge of Brian but then remembered this was her t'ai chi day. Luckily I just caught her.

'Aimée! Has she left you on your own again? You should get out more, you know, like me. Join a class. What's up, anyway? I'm just about to go out the door.'

'To t'ai chi. I did remember, Granny. I don't just telephone you when I'm fed up, you know.'

'Not always. Now, I've no time for idle chit-chat or I'll miss my bus. What did you really want?'

You can't fool the Granny.

'OK,' I conceded. 'Who's Brian?'

'Brian who?'

'No, who's Brian?'

'What are you talking about?'

'Has Mammy mentioned a Brian to you?'

'No, not that I remember, and you know your Mammy

can't hold her own water. You're getting paranoid, Aimée. Anyway, why shouldn't she have a significant other?'

Granny's weakness is daytime reality television. Especially anything American. She prefers her angst sun-bronzed and toned.

Change of tactic.

'Granny, did Mammy ever mention if my da had a vasectomy?'

Silence. Was there a code of *omertà* operating here?

'Aimée, are you all right? You're not, are you?'

'Granny, I'm fine. I'm just excited. I'm taking part in this twinning project with Knockgorey. It's a big school in Foxrock and we have to draw up a personal profile. It's got me thinking about family issues,' I ended lamely.

'What exactly happens?'

I *knew* she'd be drawn in. Healthy curiosity is a characteristic passed down the female line.

'Well, we get paired with a pupil about our own age. They pick someone they think we might get on with and we contact each other by email. Or online. You know, on the computer, where I'm always on to the girls and anyone who's online can join in the conversation and it's free and the little smiley faces pop up and stuff?'

'Aimée McCourt-Logan, you are talking to a Silver Surfer. A bit of respect, please. I do clip art. Or is it art house? Something like that.'

'Sorry, Granny. It's all about sharing experiences. Like, I'll be telling her about my life here and she'll be telling me about Ireland under the Celtic Tiger and stuff. And then we meet up.'

'Well, don't build yourself up too much, Aimée, love. The Celtic Tiger has gone out the cat flap. I must go! Bye!'

I wondered where she heard that one? I made a mental note to remember that for the Da in case he could use it in an article on the double-dip recession.

Time to get going.

I went into the bedroom to pull on my black combats and sweatshirt – the nearest equivalent to PJs – and found them coated with cat hairs, courtesy of you-know-who's mid-morning nap. My new pink lippy had gone the same way as the lenses – straight across the floor and under the furniture – leaving an interesting, possibly indelible pattern alongside last night's juice. Rainbow is quite possibly the only cat in Ireland with undiagnosed attention deficit hyperactivity disorder. Mentally, I added 'stain remover' to 'sports bra 34C/D' on my shopping list.

Phone on. Check texts. One from Bree:

> Hi at Saralous cn u rply thr – do u no whr cn gt 6 aqua ra-ras 8/10 + 12 pompoms aqua/whte n sndtrak f Sprngsteens gtest hts b4 3?

She will confuse text, speed writing, email and chat. Like adults do, only different.

Another, from Rebekah:

> Taking kids to McDs at 3. meet me therc if u r in town.

That'd put Fiona off motherhood for sure, if it weren't already too late.

Suddenly I realised what I was – loathsome, mean-minded and jealous. Jealous of a potential embryo, for God's sake. And I knew, and my friends knew, that, whatever else, the Mammy and Daddy, eccentric, infuriating and embarrassing though they are, had not gone a day since they parted without putting me first. More than ten years, or 36,500 days. And all I could think was that I didn't want to share them with a partner or potential sprog. When, in all probability, I'd be leaving home in a few years. Too many chilling thoughts. Check my inbox, then switch off.

A quick tidy, so I could find the chair at my computer desk, and I logged on. Emails first.

Three junk: two offering me cheap supplies of Viagra and Cialis – is there no decency left? – and a third promoting investments in gold bullion. Delete, delete, delete.

Facebook. I checked it last thing last night, but just in case ... Let's see ... news feed. Most recent. Daily horoscope for Sagittarius: lucky colour: green. Lucky time: 8 a.m. Slept through it. Typical.

One new friend request.

And then I saw her name on screen for the first time and I knew. My virtual friend. My social network sister.

Accept.

Check her home page. Quick.

Caoimhe Cassidy.

Her profile pic was Tigger. No clue there. I mean, who doesn't like Winnie the Pooh?

One new message.

Click.

Hi, Aimée. Hope this is you! My name's Caoimhe Cassidy (as in Knockgorey, Foxrock) and I'm not supposed to know you're my twin because your school hasn't officially approved the twinning matches proposed by our Mr Lynch yet,

```
but Nick let slip when he was getting me
into my taxi after drama last night that
I'm paired with an Aimée McCourt-Logan
and I THINK this must be you. I hope so!
Is that your cat? He's so cute. If
you're reading this on a Saturday you
must be as bored as I am ... message me
back!! x
```

Now, I am by nature suspicious of anyone who purports to be so interested in a person they haven't even met. But I was curious. Was Nick Mr Lynch? Why was drama on a Friday night? Were they doing a show? And why was Nick – Mr Lynch? – helping her into a taxi? There's only one reason why any of my classmates need to be helped into a taxi on a Friday night and it's a very different kind of drama.

Still, I liked her initiative. They'd got my name right, too. That's how she found me so quickly, I expect. Aimée, not Amy or Aimi. Aimée, as in the French for beloved. So Knockgorey paid attention to spelling, which was more than some of my teachers did. Or relations, come to that.

Caoimhe Cassidy. It sounded good, like a folk singer or maybe a newsreader. My twin. Not a pen pal with its connotations of sad loners exchanging bilingual birthday cards and costume dolls.

I gathered Rainbow on to my lap for a cuddle and to-gether we set about messaging back Caoimhe Cassidy. Maybe we could chat online later. Saturday was looking up.

Chapter Four

I scrutinised the profile page before me. No relationship status. Goes to Knockgorey College, lives in Foxrock, County Dublin. So far, so predictable.

```
           Into The Smiths,
             The Wanted,
            Justin Bieber
          (naturally), Hendrix,
    Billie Holliday (I think that's what's
called an eclectic mix), witty chick-lit,
weepy DVDs, DRAMA XX, Maeve Higgins, HWBs
in winter, tandoori, Häagen-Dazs (Dulce de
Leche).
```

I wish! Either fat and proud or a natural skinny.

```
Pets: I wish!
```

Fussy parents?

Various 'Knockgorey is SOOOO cool – not'-type comments. And uploaded pics of what seemed to be a pantomime with a cast of thousands. Among them was, presumably, Caoimhe Cassidy.

```
Email address:
caoimheimneverwrong@mail.net
Star sign: Sagittarius.
```

An astral twin, too! It had to be a portent of good. Not that I believe in horoscopes. But the omens were promising. I just knew this was a significant moment in my life. In years to come, my old friend Caoimhe Cassidy and I would reminisce over this moment – stop, Aimée. Take a chill pill. If you message back, straight away, you'll look sad. A bit of a loser.

It was much more important to deal with the to-do list, at speed. A quick perusal of the delights of the lingerie counter before joining the Da and all the other shopaholics' partners as they sipped lukewarm lager and berated our national team for losing at whatever sport. Then back online with a clear conscience and a dutiful nod towards a meaningful Saturday.

I glanced at the time and saw it was already half past two – damn.

I fairly sprinted to the door when my mobile rang, shouting 'On my way' into the orifice of what I trusted was the Da's on the other end of the phone. I paused only to shut Rainbow in the bathroom where his varied bodily functions and personal habits can best be

accommodated in my absence. In no time, I was bounc-
ing into the back seat beside the Da and Fiona, as a
patently psychotic taxi driver trimmed a good two
minutes off his best time round the route. Such close
quarters are not conducive to carrying out a subtle line
of enquiry to ascertain whether the Da's paramour is in
what Gran says used to be euphemistically called 'an interesting condition'. Still, duty called, and nothing
ventured ...

'How's work, Fiona?'

'Frantic. It's been a bit of a mad week.'

I know you were at the hospital.

'Had you a lot of appointments and stuff?'

(I don't even know what she does, really.)

'Yeah, I was out and about a lot this week. I'm wrecked.'

Rebekah says extreme tiredness is one of the sure signs
of early pregnancy.

'Should you be taking it easy then?' I asked guilelessly.

She paused for maybe a few seconds too long.

'That's what weekends are for, isn't it, Aimée? Just
chilling out.'

Non-committal. A politic answer.

'I don't know where your mum gets her energy from.
To work weekends, I mean.'

'She loves her work. She'd never give it up for – well,
anything.'

Not motherhood, for sure.

'Shopping,' the Da interjected, 'is one of the most
stressful leisure pursuits known to man.'

'Yeah, but not to woman, right, Aimée?'

I pick up on this bonding stuff. Maybe if I share a
little she will reciprocate? Pulling what I hoped was a

mildly humorous grimace, I confided, 'I've got to get a new sports bra. I hate shopping for bras with a passion.'

'Oh, do you? I quite enjoy it, actually.'

Why did I say that? What if she offered to come with me? Right into the cubicle? I would die of embarrassment.

'It always puts me in a good mood,' Fiona chatted on. 'You know, treating myself to new lingerie.'

Too much information. I looked to the Da. But survival instinct had kicked in and his eyes were fixed firmly, if helplessly, on the road ahead.

The taxi screeched to a halt on a double yellow line beside the entrance to the town's main shopping centre. Which is conveniently located opposite a pub with a widescreen TV, where happy hour on a Saturday morphs seamlessly into happy day and then happy night. The Da fumbled for change.

'I'll be no more than half an hour,' Fiona called over her shoulder, blowing him a kiss as she strode purposefully towards the reinforced glass doors. I trotted along beside her and together we pushed our way into the frenzied mêlée of Saturday afternoon social shopping.

We stopped at the foot of the escalator.

'I'm away in here, Aimée,' Fiona said, pointing in the general direction of a Boots. 'I've got to stock up on, you know, women's stuff. The sort of thing I could never send Eamonn for.'

No, I didn't know. Tampons? Definitely not pregnant. Stretch-mark cream? Nipple shields? I realised I was staring much too intently at her chest area.

'OK, then, Aimée. I'll see you later, in the pub, maybe?'

Go for it, Aimée. Take courage.

'Rebekah's mum shops in Boots,' I proffered. 'You know her. Mrs O'Hara. She's very pregnant,' I added after a pause.

'Everyone shops in Boots.' Fiona shrugged.

'She says they do lovely baby clothes.'

Still no response. The desperation in my voice was palpable.

'You know Mrs O'Hara, Fiona. Don't you?'

'Yes, I saw her this week, in fact. At the hospital. She can't have long to go now.'

Pause. And what were you doing at the antenatal clinic, Fiona?

Another long pause.

'Are you looking for a present for the baby, Aimée?'

What?

'Mrs O'Hara's baby,' Fiona added.

Did my expression give me away?

'I'll come round with you if you want and help you pick something –'

'It's all right,' I replied, too quickly, stepping on to the escalator and bounding up two steps at a time.

Don't confide in me then. See if I care. I'm only the half-sister in waiting. Or is it step-? If I'm anything in waiting, that is.

I briefly considered doubling back down and stalking her round the chemist's. Then I caught myself on. A direct question would have been simpler. But not even I had the front to ask it. Not yet, anyway. And there was no point asking the Da. He probably wouldn't have known. Onwards and upwards.

Wafting through the swing doors of the biggest department store in town, I turned a blind eye to the sign warning that my bosoms are almost certainly among the eighty-five per cent supported (or not) by the wrong cup size. I found a white sports bra, D cup. Better safe than sorry and I could cut out the incriminating label when I got home. It didn't even look that big. I couldn't possibly be a DD, could I?

Then on to the pound shop for stain remover. Passing McDs I saw the O'Hara dynasty arranged in sequential order, their smeared and smiling faces testament to the adhesive and mood-enhancing powers of a Happy Meal. I called over to Rebekah, who was dispensing red sauce sachets and general wisdom, and heard that Bree was looking for me.

I popped my head round the door of the lounge bar beside the taxi rank, declined a Diet Coke, pleading urgent matters at Riverview, unspecified, and was at the front of the bus queue within twenty-five minutes, which is no mean feat.

I spent the bus ride mentally composing my scintillating and engaging reply to Caoimhe which would make me sound like – well, the sort of person I would want as a Facebook friend, if you see what I mean.

Back at the ranch, I got down to the real thing.

```
Hi Caoimhe,
Great to hear from you.

Just back from the shops. Free gaff
tonight as my mum's at a conference and
my da and his partner are in the pub.
```

No, that sounded all wrong. I highlighted and deleted the words from my computer screen. How about this?

Hi Caoimhe,
Just got your message!

What a lie! Delete.

Shopping in town — SOOO boring! Not like
Dublin, I bet. Mum's at a conference so
I've a free house tonight.

That was better.

My form teacher, Mizz Hardy, is clearly
a fantasist, as she told us we'd be
selected for this project according to
the vibrancy of our personal statements.
She never said your Mr Lynch had it all
sorted. So thanks for the heads up on
what's really going on.

I'm really glad we've been twinned.

Talk soon,
Aimée

Send.

Rainbow's stomach rumbled and I remembered that I hadn't eaten since breakfast. So much for the healthy snack every four hours to keep the metabolic rate at its peak. Time for a microwaved Mammy meal. And a banana, and a few squares of seventy per cent cocoa solids dark chocolate to boost the old endorphins. Maybe an isotonic sports drink. (How can it be low-calorie *and* give you energy?)

Then maybe a bit of channel-hopping.

Maybe a few sit-ups or an exercise DVD.

Maybe a few gossipy phone calls.
Maybe.
It was Saturday evening, for God's sake. The world was out enjoying itself.
Except me.

*

Bored. I was in my PJs, cleansed, toned and moisturised and with nothing to do.

After many failed attempts to entertain myself after dinner, I found myself back in front of the computer screen in search of a virtual social life.

Imagine if I could really tell it like it is. Like, let's see … I idly opened my email account. Click. New message.

```
From: aimeemcclogan@derry.com
To: caoimheimneverwrong@mail.net
```

So, let the two-finger typing commence:

```
Hi Caoimhe,
I rushed home from the town today after
buying a surgical garment masquerading
as a sports bra which makes me look
ample - that's the only word for it -
then spent ages composing the sort of
reply that I hope would make you think
I'm uber-cool.

Yeah, well. It's not like I'd actually
send this email.

Now it's gone eight o'clock, the telly's
crap and the free house is just that -
```

free. Apart from me and Rainbow (he's
the refuge cat) sitting in on a Saturday
night at age fifteen and eight
(respectively). Sad or what? You haven't
replied so I expect you're out and about
in Dublin's pubs and clubs. Like a
normal person. Even my da's in the pub
and he's long past his sell-by date.

Yours despondently,
Aimée

The doorbell shattered my concentration. Simultaneously my mobile rang and I saw Bree flashing on caller display.

'Let me in, let me in, let me in,' she sang. Yes, sang. OK, chanted.

Time to log off.

Oh. My. God.

Message sent.

I had sent the bloody message. Instinctively. By mistake.

My useful life at Castle Grove was over.

I wanted to crawl away and die. Immediately. Instead I pulled on my dressing gown and answered the insistent doorbell …

Bree stood on the doorstep, pompoms akimbo, slender thighs mottled because of the cold.

'Surprise!'

'Surprise,' I echoed weakly.

'I thought I'd come round on my way home so you can help me do my maths coursework.'

She breezed past in a flurry of ra-ra frills. As she headed towards my room I saw she was displaying the legend 'GoPual' on her T-shirt, between her skinny shoulder blades.

'No, you've come round so I can *do* your maths coursework,' I corrected her with not a little predictable sarcasm. 'And how can I if you've come straight from cheerleading?' I said, noting the absence of maths coursework on her person.

But she was already ferreting beneath a pile of papers and emerged bearing aloft the relevant poly pocket.

'I took the precaution of leaving it here yesterday. Questions eleven to fifteen, inclusive. It'll not even stretch you. Promise.'

She was smug.

'Besides, I know Clio is out until God knows when at her gender thingy and Rebekah is babysitting – like, what's new? So I thought you'd be glad of some company. I'd hate to think of you sitting in alone on a Saturday night,' she added philanthropically as I consulted the offending pages.

'You can do them later,' she went on generously. 'It'll give you something to look forward to.'

Dear God, had it come to this? An object of pity and not yet sixteen?

'I'm freezing. I'll make us a bite to eat. You look a bit peaky,' she continued, gravitating towards the kitchen. 'You're supposed to eat every four hours, you know. To keep your metabolic thingy whatever. Or maybe it's your blood sugar. Something. Come in and talk to me while I'm cooking.'

'Making toast, you mean.'

'That's cooking. So, give us your craic. I am *so* low in carbs after all the aerobic and cardio I did today, prancing up and down that pitch,' she gabbled on. 'I hope you're not taking this healthy eating regime too seriously, Aimée? I mean, you'll never be a size eight, like, not with your frame.'

'Backside, you mean. And boobs.'

'I said frame. You're more Beyoncé, aren't you? I mean she is *so* hot. Personally I think you're cursed with a slow metabolism, or an under-active thyroid,' she confided. Her diagnosis was possibly gleaned from Clio. Now she was opening the peanut butter and the chocolate hazelnut spread in greedy anticipation of a sandwichfest. Why were they discussing my endomorphism? And behind my back, too?

'It's one of those things. Like lazy sperm. Live with it, y'know? Want a slice?'

'Well … one slice, peanut butter only.'

'No butter?'

'Peanut butter *is* butter.'

'Suppose it is,' she agreed distractedly, liberally lathering both on her bottom deck.

'Who or what is GoPual?' I venture.

'What? Don't ask me quiz questions; how would I know?'

'I am merely quoting what is emblazoned across the back of your T-shirt so I assume it is of some significance to you,' I muttered as she added a good three centimetres of chocolate and licked the knife.

'What are you on about? Ahh …' Realisation dawned and in a manoeuvre worthy of a burlesque queen she swivelled round the offending garment so it faced forwards. 'Typical bloody Carly.'

'Got her vowels transposed?' I suggested, but I was met with a blank stare of incomprehension. She is in basic English, like I said. Meow.

'It's supposed to say Go Paul,' she explained unnecessarily. 'I knew there wasn't room for a space between the o and the P, but what can you expect from Carly?'

'And what did she do with Go Orlando?' I mused.

'What? Oh God no, she is *so* over him. He's yesterday's news. History. *Finito.*'

The toaster swallowed two more slices.

'Ish Bwndn,' she elucidated through a mouthful of toast.

'That'll be Bwndn Reilly, then.'

From 12O. Has just about mastered the art of walking vertically. A bitch? *Moi?*

'Thash what I shed.' The starving one swallowed. 'He's all right, isn't he?'

I threw my eyes up.

'Aimée, you are so … fussy! Honestly, is it any wonder that – '

'That I'm single and sitting in on a Saturday night?' She looked embarrassed. Mildly, but embarrassed nonetheless.

'Noo, what I meant was, well …'

'Beggars can't be choosers? Bree, shut it before you really *do* hurt my feelings, OK?'

'Oh, Aimée, don't be like that.'

And she threw her arms round my neck in a way that has disarmed many a pubescent misogynist.

'It's just, maybe, you know, you need to experiment. I think you should get out more.'

Bree *and* Gran? Both? In one day?

Why not just say it: get a life, Aimée.

I was saved from compounded patronising by the shriek of her mobile.

'GoPual,' I suggested.

'What? Oh, yes, haha, hello sweetie ...'

Sweetie? Dear God, had she neither dignity nor discernment? Sexy – maybe. Cool – arguably. Sweet? Not by any rational definition could that overgrown streak of emerging manhood be described as sweet.

I made my own toast.

After intermittent shrieking, giggling, chewing and affirming, Bree put her hand over the receiver.

'What time will Clio be back at?'

'Late. I dunno. *No!* No way!'

'Clio wouldn't mind,' she said with a pout. 'I'll text her.'

'Her phone will be off; she's working. And no. Full stop. Non-negotiable, OK? What's wrong with your house?' I added.

It was bad enough sitting in alone on a Saturday night in mental anguish over having sent a stupid email to a prospective Facebook friend and exchange twin without having your BF and her bloke cavorting in the next room. Our walls are so thin it's virtually indecent.

'Sorcha,' she said with considerable gravitas, 'is entertaining.'

A dinner party? A coven? The troops?

No, apparently a twenty-eight-year-old exchange student who goes by the predictable and probably assumed name of Miguel.

'He has a stall on the Ramblas,' Bree added as her beloved waited behind her clamped-on palm to hear his fate. 'Anyway, Sorcha kind of hinted ... well, she told me not to be back before midnight ... if I could help it. I could even stay overnight ...'

I felt a warm rush of affection and gratitude for a mother who, though undoubtedly unconventional, is more likely to offer advice on when to come home than when not to.

'His house?' I suggested with more hope than conviction.

'No privacy and it's a kip. Well, not exactly a kip. But you know what they say about Sycamore Heights.'

She didn't wait for my consent.

'Sweetie? Yes, it's fine, I'll just give you the address. Now write it down for the taxi, OK? It's number 1A. No, 1*A*. Tell you what, I'll order it for you, that'll be quicker.'

I disappeared into the loo before the conversation descended into the you-hang-up-first-no-you-do exchange which must cost her a fair few pounds in credit each time.

I resigned myself to an even quieter night in solitary (apart from Rainbow who would, I predicted, dislike GoPual) when a voice called through the (thin) door.

'Aimée? Can you lend us a fiver for the taxi? I'm skint.'

'Take a tenner.' I was all munificence. 'Then you can order one home as well. For a quarter to twelve, OK?'

Rainbow and I needed our beauty sleep.

I left the computer on sleep and, with Rainbow curled in a furry arc around my head, and, worn out by the emotional turmoil of the day, I slept.

Well, tried to.

10.30.

Ringringring. Doorbell.

GoPual (I must stop this before it sticks) and Bree (his paramour with the turbo-charged metabolism) had gone for chips and locked themselves out. Naturally. They hadn't wakened me to see if I wanted anything because I 'looked so snug'.

Healthy eating by default.

10.55. Just dozing off.

Taptaptap.

No, thank you, I do not want three leftover chicken nuggets which have been dunked in that Irish takeaway staple, taco sauce.

10.57.

Taptaptap.

Nor does Rainbow, thank you. He is on an elimination diet to find out if he is, as Clio suspects, gluten intolerant.

11.05.

Ringringring. Landline.

It was the Da.

'Just wanted to check, you know, that you're all right on your own. I promised your mother I'd give you a ring. Is she back yet?'

'No. Not yet.'

'Are you OK then, on your own? You're not lonely or anything?'

'What makes you assume I'm on my own?'

Pause. I liked it.

'Aimée. No, I didn't … I mean, is Rebekah over with you?'

'No. She's babysitting. As usual.'

Longer pause. I loved it.

'Ah, right.'

'Yeah.'

'Aimée ...'

'Yeah?'

'Have you a friend over? I don't mind, you know. We don't mind.'

'No, it's a gang of armed and masked intruders doing a tiger robbery – Da, Da, sorry, bad joke, I know, yes, I know you worry, yes, sorry, oh for God's sake, it's Bree and her beloved. Yes. That's right, they have no home to go to.' Unsuccessfully attempting copulation by the sound of it. 'OK. Night, Da. Love you, too. Night.'

Were you alone, Da? And was it any of my business?

It still felt like it was.

11.27.

Taptaptap.

'C'm in, Bree.'

'I've rung for our taxi. Paul has to be home by midnight at the latest.'

'Mm.'

'The dispatcher said it'll be about ten minutes. I told him to use ringback.'

'Mm.'

'And he'll ring your house phone. I hope you don't mind. It's just, I'm nearly out of credit.'

'Mm.'

'Thanks. You know, for the space. For letting me give Sorcha some space.'

'No probs.'

'Aimée?'

'Mm?'

I could hear her rummaging around my desk.

'Leave all that stuff, will you?' I beg. 'I'll bring your maths into school on Monday.'

'OK.'

I could hear her clicking on the PC.

'Aimée, don't worry if you feel like sleeping a lot.'

I didn't. I was worrying about idiot friends keeping me awake.

'Sorcha says lack of sleep can make you fat. Holistically. Or maybe metabolically. I'm not sure. Fat anyway. Not that –'

'Thanks.'

'Aimée.'

'Mm?'

'I think … you know … I think Paul might be The One. Really.'

'Paul?'

Thank God I didn't say GoPual.

'Ssh! He'll hear you. He's only in the bog. You said it yourself: you could spit through these walls. Sorcha says that's why she hates new houses.'

'The Da's the same,' I muttered.

Clio and I have lived here since our address was Plot 1A. And she is happy to have Put Her Stamp On It.

A shriek. Horror or excitement? Over architectural construction?

'Oh my God. Aimée, get up! Look!'

I extracted myself from my furry nightcap, much to the furry nightcap's displeasure, and sat up.

'Aimée!'

I switched on the main light.

Bree sat, transfixed, in front of the computer screen.

'Are you reading my emails? No. You're in my Facebook messages –'

'Ssh! Aimée, look.'

She pulled me onto the chair beside her.

Right before our eyes. The most gorgeous bloke I had seen in weeks. Months even.

I looked again.

Make that, quite possibly, ever.

'Who's he?' I asked the obvious.

'How do I know? It's a jpeg on a message in your inbox. So he must be a friend. He must have sent it to you, mustn't he?'

Ringring.

The house phone. Two rings, then rang off. It was her taxi ringback. Thank you, Lord.

It was my turn to shriek. 'There's your taxi. You'd better go. Quick! They won't wait round on a Saturday night.'

Taptaptap through the thin door

'Bree, love, taxi. They won't wait round on a Saturday night.'

'I KNOW! COMING!'

She grabbed her bag and threw me a departing glance which seemed to say, Who the hell is he, why is he sending you his picture, where have you been hiding him, why have you been hiding him, tell me more.

'I could let Paul take this one.'

'And go home to his mammy in Sycamore Heights unchaperoned? Never.'

I steered her, protesting, in the direction of the front door.

'I wouldn't hear of it. After all, it is Saturday night. You'd wait ages for another taxi,' I smiled sweetly, shutting the door behind the happy couple. Firmly.

Wide awake now, sensors flaring, I sat down in front of the screen. Thick, dark hair with a hint of auburn – not ginger, not even remotely. Deep green eyes. Really green, not the watery blue-green-grey indigenous Irish shade. A wide smile, not cheeky, not cocky, not forced, not poser-y. Just … happy. A genuinely happy smile. I smiled back. Seventeen? Maybe a year either way.

Then I saw, for the first time, a pale face to the right and slightly behind his. Safe in his shadow. An oval face, pretty rather than gorgeous, surrounded by layers of dark blonde hair.

Taking care to save it in my documents, I went back to my inbox.

From: caoimheimneverwrong@mail.net
To: aimeemcclogan@derry.com
22.45

I clicked on the attachment. I felt a chill in the pit of my stomach. Not only had my prospective virtual friend replied to my cretinous communication, she had added insult to injury by forwarding a picture of herself and her bloke. She might as well have captioned the email 'Unattainable'.

What *was* it captioned?
Darren and me, the garden, Foxrock, August 2011.
Darren. Darren and Caoimhe. Caoimhe and Darren.
She probably wouldn't have time to be much of a virtual friend. Too loved up.

Not like me.
Not at *all* like me. Ever.
Better read what she says, masochist that I am.

```
Good to hear from u on what's clearly a
busy day.
```

Sarcastic cow.

```
Not like here.
```

Oh?

```
Hope you don't think I'm a bit sad
getting in touch at the weekend, but I'm
so BORED!! One of my BFs, Shauna, is at
pony camp.
```

Pony camp! And her style was very polite. Maybe no bad thing, looking at the illiterate witterates round here.

```
My other BF Amanda is surgically
attached to this nerdy bloke, Ronan. I
have no idea why. As for shopping in
Dublin - I wish! Have you heard of the
recession? And the EU bailout? But at
least you can take advantage of the
exchange rate when you come to visit,
which I hope you will.

Talk soon,
Caoimhe

PS Can you get into clubs and pubs in
Derry at fifteen? If so I'm on the next
bus!
```

PPS Sorry for sounding such a misery, it's been one of those days and it's that time of the month - your email cheered me up, you sound so zany and pure mad!

PPPS I know the school rules said no pictures and no Facebook (as if) and I HATE having my photo taken but I've added this one of me and my big bro Darren. It was taken in the summer so neither of us has changed much (except he's grown another inch.)

PPPPS He's the pretty one!

Darren Cassidy. Not Darren the boyfriend. Undoubtedly Darren *someone's* boyfriend, I told myself. Be still, my hormones.

Click, tiptoe.

The front door.

Clio.

A face appeared round my door.

'You're still up? Who was eating chips?'

'Bree and GoPual – Paul. They've gone,' I added un-necessarily.

'That was kind of them, to come round.'

She perched on the edge of the bed.

'Hope you weren't too bored.'

'Not at all. I was fine. Dad rang.'

'Oh. What time at?'

I paused to think.

'About eleven.'

'So he wasn't out then? I mean, it is Saturday night.'

I know the days of the week.

'What did he want?'

She got up again.

'Just to see that I was OK.'

'That's good of him. Was Fiona there?'

I shrugged.

'Dunno. They were in town earlier. In the pub. Watching the rugby.'

'Massacre of the innocents, I heard. Do you want hot chocolate? Who's he?'

I had clicked to enlarge the picture and was toying with the idea of making it my screen saver.

My mother peered at the image. Myopic? Disbelieving? I ignored this.

'No thanks. Who's Brian?'

'Aimée.'

'Seriously, who's Brian? Cliona?'

She grinned.

'Brian is a terribly serious PhD student who has attached himself to me for the duration of the conference and very possibly the rest of the term and is profiling me for his casebook. He gave me a lift today, as you know. It was very kind of him and Jilly and I bought him lunch. In the refectory.'

'Canteen.'

'Canteen, then. He gave us both a lift home, too,' my mother went on. 'Not that it's really any of your business, Aimée.'

'No.'

'And now he and the younger element have gone on to the disco at the staff common room and I am going to my bed.'

'So am I, Mammy. Night.'

She gave me a hug.

'Sure you don't want anything?'

'Well, maybe just a small hot chocolate. Low calorie,' I added quickly.

'What other kind do I buy? Ordinary or hazelnut?'

'Ordinary, please.'

I shut down the computer.

Night night, Caoimhe Cassidy. Night night, Darren Cassidy. Talk soon.

And after that email! It was hardly me at my most inspiring. You never can tell. Nowt as queer as folk, as the Granny says.

I snuggled under the duvet. Rainbow reclaimed his rightful place. Clio brought in a huge frothy hot chocolate.

'His name's Darren. Darren Cassidy,' I told her in what I hoped was a confidently off-hand way. 'He's a Dub.'

'I thought I didn't recognise him from Castle Grove,' she mused.

'Definitely not. Most definitely not. Night, Mam.'

Night night.

Chapter Five

I am sure the Almighty knew what She was doing when She created Sunday but thus far into my life its *raison d'être* remains a divine mystery to me. Slow Sunday, a non-day. In fact, the rest of the next week was much the same so there's no sense in inflicting my boredom and the tedious minutiae of daily life at 1A Riverview/12G Castle Grove on anyone other than those for whom it is inescapable reality.

Four more days of my life were preoccupied with trivia. The next event of any note came at Friday morning's form class, forty-five fun-filled minutes which allegedly start the wind-down for the weekend for all but the most sadistic members of the teaching profession. Mizz was still energised from her brainstorming session at the charity fundraising event and overflowing with Can Do Attitude. I surveyed the wound-down faces around me and pitied her innocence.

Barry actually appeared to be in a coma. Or at least a trance-like state. Possibly substance-induced, possibly natural.

'The twinning process is complete! The selection is over and this morning those of you who have been selected will be put in touch officially with your Knockgorey counterpart!'

Officially? Who was she getting at? I knew Bree had mouthed about Caoimhe's pre-emptive strike. Maybe I should have been quicker to erase her 'Aimée hearts Darren' graffiti in the second-floor bogs, but, hell, it added to my air of mystery – assuming everyone discounted the possibility that it was that nerdy weed Darren Dickson in 9V. Nobody could have believed I was that desperate.

'And I am counting on those of you who, for whatever reason, have not been twinned to support this class venture in every way you can,' she added. 'We don't want anyone to feel disappointed or excluded. Castle Grove values inclusion.'

Mizz gave me my introduction pack. It included print-outs of Caoimhe Cassidy's personal statement, contact details and an official list of Suggestions of Topics to Discuss. I scanned it quickly.

There was also a TBC list of planned events and a time framework. It included a family-friendly Hallowe'en carnival induction weekend. Well, overnight stay, since Hallowe'en would fall on a Monday. Typical.

And if successful, a two-centre Festive Fun Christmas Conference with Seasonal Special Events (embracing those of all religious/ethnic traditions and none). Inclusive, like Mizz said.

But Hallowe'en! Knockgorey coming to Derry! Oh My Lord, and just six weeks away! Was there a waiting list for liposuction?

The rest of the briefing flew past in a blur. My peripheral vision registered that Patricia Mooney had a twinning pack (of course) and so did Carly, Steven McQuillan (eh?) and the usual keenly motivated and effusively PC suspects.

Mizz invited us to add our carnival ideas to the brainstorm board. Bree's cheerleading team had morphed into majorettes – Bree's Babes – and they were right up there, naturally. Patricia Wannabe Mooney had suggested a celebrity lookalike/Stars in Their Eyes competition. A fancy dress pageant was a must, of course. The rest of the empty space quickly filled with reasonably sensible suggestions including a historical ghost tour, sponsored haunt, five-a-side gender-friendly soccer slam, cross-community face painting and balloon modelling – just the delights to impress a bevy of sophisticated Transition Years from Dublin. I don't think. The full list, we were told, would be on the noticeboard by lunchtime.

*

'Costumes,' Bree decreed as we huddled round my screen saver that afternoon. Majorettes' practice had been cancelled as Carly had a dental appointment, no one had yet sourced the Springsteen track (memo: ask the Da) and, besides, it was chucking it down.

'I'm still wearing your yellow and black ... I am, amn't I?'

Rebekah's lower lip trembled. She doesn't get out much. The Firewall *matters*.

'Course you are,' I reassured the trembling one. 'It's all sorted – and Bree's wearing –'

'Fancy dress, you eejits. For the pageant,' Bree interrupted.

'I thought you meant tomorrow night. The Firewall.'

'The Firewall is history.'

Rebekah's lip trembled again.

'No offence, Beks, but it's a bit ... juvenile, isn't it? I think we need to start planning our Hallowe'en cozzies. We want them to be really brilliant.' This from the dancing queen of Firewall?

Then came the killer blow. 'Paul and I,' Bree paused for effect, 'may not be going to the Firewall. It's really just for singles, isn't it? I mean,' she went on, 'you don't get many couples there, do you? Carly says Brendan says his friends aren't bothered going – none of the Sycamore Heights ones are.'

'They're not all couples, though.'

'But you know what I mean, Aimée. It's not our thing.'

'It was last week,' Rebekah spoke quietly. She was glum.

So was I. A Firewall without Bree strutting her stuff in the dance-off was not the same.

The traitor sensed our feelings of betrayal. 'I mean,' she appealed, gesturing to the screen saver, 'you're not going to meet the likes of him at the Firewall, are you? It'll be full of creepy wee Year 9s perving on us and pretending they're off their faces on a can of Cidona. Come on, it'll be like doing bog duty on the juniors at break time.'

The silence told her that, for some of us, it wouldn't. *Ringringring.* Saved by her mobile.

'Hi, sweets, yes ... yes ... hold on, just a minute ... Got to go,' Bree hissed at us. 'We can talk about it later, OK?'

She left in such a hurry she forgot to leave her latest maths coursework for me to do over the weekend.

*

'Are we too old for this craic?'

Saturday night had finally arrived and Beks and I were getting ready for the Firewall. Rebekah stood beside the bed, facing her reflection in the full-length mirror. With her hair brushed loose and gleaming, and wearing what was, in its last incarnation, my yellow and black, altered to size, she looked petite and radiant.

'Of course we're not,' replied the dark and bulbous reflection looming behind her. 'Not that you're ever going to meet anyone nearly good enough for you at the Firewall, Beks.'

Then I got embarrassed when she replied, 'Nor are you, Aimée. Don't put yourself down in front of Bree. She can be an idiot sometimes, you know.'

'Only sometimes?'

And we both laughed.

'Seriously. I'm not looking to meet anyone. Certainly not what Bree would call "The One",' Rebekah went on earnestly. 'All I want is a really good night out. A chance to let my hair down, if you like. No pun intended. I want not to have to worry about kids and coursework and dilated cervixes for a couple of hours. Speaking of which,' and she took a print-out from her overnight bag, 'I nearly forgot to give you these.'

I saw the title, 'Vasectomy: Yes or No?' I'd forgotten all about that.

'It's off a really good website,' she added. 'I use it all the time for my Biology. It might answer a few of your questions.'

'Thanks.' I forced a smile. Thanks for reminding me. But it wasn't your fault.

'Now,' my personal stylist insisted, 'that outfit does nothing for you. Too baggy, too black. Embrace your curves, Aimée. Clio!'

'No!' I squealed. In vain.

Powerless against the combined forces of mother and mate, I was made over, big style.

Hair straightened and fixed over one shoulder. Make-up that was, frankly, gothic. One of Clio's multicoloured retro silk tunics, my own best (tightest) black jeans, Clio's killer heel gladiators and, as the fashionista in me says, we were hot to trot.

'I'll order the taxi to wait at the top of the hill at five to midnight,' Clio informed us. 'And remember: any hassle, ring me.'

I threw a farewell glance at the screen saver.

Night night, Caoimhe Cassidy. Talk, officially, to-morrow. Night night, Darren Cassidy. Wish you were here. And, if you were, would you look twice at me?

From: aimeemcclogan@derry.com
To: caoimheimneverwrong@mail.net
01.23

```
Hi Caoimhe,
It's now gone Sunday and I haven't heard
from you so I'll take the initiative and
write the first formal communication
since we were officially twinned.
```

'Socially inept,' whispered Rebekah. 'Way too formal.'
Agreed. Delete.

```
Just home from the Firewall disco, the
monthly highlight of our social
calendar.
```

('Just' added an immediacy even if Beks and I had already
eaten our own combined bodyweight in chocolate spread
and Häagen-Dazs. After such a night, comfort eating was
not only justifiable but obligatory.)

```
The average age was about twelve (that's
Year 8 here), average height (male)
about 5ft, average height (female, plus
platforms) 5ft 6ins, and my best friend
Rebekah (who's here with me) and I felt
like overdressed childminders.

Some of our 9V laughed at us! US! Can you
believe it? Beks swears she heard one wee
lad chanting OAPs, OAPs, OAPs ...

In the absence of our own dancing queen,
my other best friend Bree Harley, due to
personal circumstances (loved up), the
dance-off was won by a thirteen-year-old
break-dancing Italian on an exchange
```

```
visit who, I suspect, was not in the
grip of a natural high.

As it was, Rebekah spent most of her
night chatting to Tom Harrison of 12R who
was there chaperoning his precocious
babe-magnet of a twelve-year-old brother,
Griffin. I've never really talked to Tom.
He always seems very serious and, well, a
bit withdrawn but Beks says he's really
sound. She says he never comes over to
talk to us because he finds Bree 'loud
and scary' and me 'intimidating'!
```

'Intimidating!'

'That's getting to you, Aimée, isn't it? Maybe I shouldn't have said ... but I didn't want you to think Tom is stuck-up.'

'It's quite all right.' I assumed chilly disregard. 'The Mammy has warned me about men like that. They're personally inadequate. They feel threatened by strong women.'

'No, he just said he found you a bit –'

'Leave it,' I said through gritted teeth.

Back to the communiqué.

```
Our only consolation is that Bree, Paul,
Carly and Brendan together with their
dysfunctional hangers-on, Infectious
Mickey Martin and Brainless Barry
Bradley, spent over an hour queueing
outside Jaguar (chav nightclub) in the
rain only to be turned away as even
```

```
their learning-limited bouncers couldn't
accept the blatantly fake ID. Then they
had to wait the best part of another
hour for a taxi.
```

'Does that make us sound like two bitches?'
'Absolutely,' Rebekah nodded. 'Carry on.'

```
We are delighted that Castle Grove is
offering an alternative to the Samhain
Firewall in the form of a Hallowe'en
Carnival and can't wait to meet you then.
My mum (Clio) will be delighted to host
you and has emailed your Mr Lynch twice
without reply. (She said to mention that.)

Talk soon and see you quite soon,
Your virtual friend,
Aimée.
```

'Cringey?'
'Yeah,' Rebekah agreed, 'but send it anyway. It's different. You can't just go online with "Wossup?" or "Hi babes wot's happnin?" She's most probably in her bed. And Rainbow's tired. He needs his sleep and he won't settle until we do.'

```
Message sent.
```

*

It was a slower than usual Sunday. Attempted to self-motivate with a to-do list followed by a 'Going Up, Going Down,' as seen in all the best colour weekend supplements. Purely to amuse self.

Felicity McCall

To Do

1
Wash, tumble dry, iron, dishes

2
Search for missing earring (Aimée)

3
Search for missing earring (Rebekah)

4
Study vasectomy literature and take
any necessary follow-up action

5
Bree's maths (she dropped it over yesterday, oh joy)

6
My maths

7
Check for signs of Mrs O'Hara's labour
(NB Google Braxton Hicks??)

8

Swap diaries with Mammy

9

Better still, swop diaries with Mammy

For the coming week

10

Check messages (hourly)

11

Check messages (half-hourly)

12

Discuss relative merits of sending Caoimhe an
airbrushed pic of me (Even a thorough scan of my home
page discloses only Rainbow's profile and joke pix)

13

Devise boot camp health and beauty regime and follow
same between now and 31.10

Now for the evaluation, as Mizz would say.

Going up this week:

Rebekah as a true friend.

Personal motivation. Goal: 10 lbs in six wks; expensive haircut (Clio?); new jeans, size 10 (Eamonn?); makeover (Rebekah); flirting tips (Bree).

Price of Hallowe'en costumes. Get started asap.

Going down this week:

Bree as a true friend.

Bree, generally.

Intimidating women (why me?).

Non-healthy food. In excess.

Checking messages more than once every half hour.

Life is never simple.

Mindless surfing of fancy-dress hire sites (some are very dodgy) was interrupted by *ringringring*. Bree.

'Your maths is done,' I told her. 'I got one wrong deliberately so as not to arouse suspicion. So it's A- or B+.'

'As if I would ring about that!'

I detected a charm offensive.

'Sooo ... tell me all the craic,' she tinkled. 'How many blokes did you get off with?'

Nothing if not direct, our Bree.

'Snogging,' I pointed out, with dignity, 'is not a competitive sport.'

'So you didn't pull then. Shame. But never mind. What about Beks?'

'Rebekah spent some quality time with Tom Harrison.'

'He's far too old to be at the Firewall.'

'He's the same age as us.'

'Exactly.'

'He was keeping an eye out for his brother.'

'Who?'

'His brother. Griffin.'

'Griffin Harrison? Is he Tom's brother? Oh my God, they're nothing like each other. Griffin's hot. I never knew they were brothers.'

'They do have the same name. He said you were scary.'

'Who? Griffin Harrison? The cheeky wee –'

'No. Tom. He told Rebekah he never comes over to talk to us cause he thinks you're scary.'

'It's his loss. Not a lot of craic there, I'd think. Mind you I did hear he has a lot of problems at home. Issues, like.'

'Ball bag. You didn't even know Griffin was his brother.'

'Just something Sorcha said one time. Forget it. Anyway, he and Beks probably chatted away about CBeebies and Micky Ds and stuff like that.'

'Griffin's twelve. He's not stupid.'

'Oh really? That's not what I heard. He is hot though. He'd pass for fifteen.'

'Bree Harley, that is obscene.'

'Sorry. Anyway, I'm spoken for. As you know.'

'How was Jaguar?'

Long pause.

'We didn't get in.'

At least she still told us the truth. Sometimes.

'I know. Just testing.'

'Bitch. How did you know?'

'The taxi driver. He recognised us and said he'd just seen our friend among a crowd of juveniles that was turned away at the door.'

I stressed the j-word.

'We would have asked him to lift you but we knew there'd have been too many of you to fit in the taxi.'

'We waited till nearly one. Can you believe that? Paul's ma went ballistic.'

'Past his bedtime?'

'I'll ignore that. Aimée, I was wondering ...'

I sensed it coming. Whatever 'it' was.

The majorettes rehearsal had been cancelled – again.

They had no music. They had dyslexic T-shirts. Two of them had mislaid their pompoms. Carly Jenkins had dropped arches. Or flat feet. Some condition that would render her ineligible for the police force/military service (perish the thought).

Patricia Mooney, who was the reserve, has dropped out to concentrate on her preparations for the Knockgorey exchange. Her mother has called in the decorators and her father, who lives at the family home (we don't take that for granted at Castle Grove), is converting the garden shed into a self-contained flat.

'You're such a good organiser, Aimée,' she wheedled. 'We need a manager.'

'Mm,' I said.

My head said no; my heart said yes. Sucker.

I clicked absently on my email account. I saw the familiar email address. Caoimheimneverwrong had sent me a reply.

'Got to go,' I called. 'I'll ring you later. After nine.'

I hung up without counting to three. Rude? Yes. But this was a priority. My virtual friend wanted to communicate with me.

Chapter
Six

From: caoimheimneverwrong@mail.net
To: aimeemcclogan@derry.com
19.20

Hi Aimée,
I'm so sorry I'm only getting round to
replying to you now but yesterday was
the day from hell.

I really wanted to send you a big cheery
message, and get a proper conversation
going on Facebook about all our news,
describing life at Knockgorey (it's
fine, really, if I'm honest) and here at
home. When I couldn't sleep last night I
even started a proper letter on proper

notepaper that Santy brought me when I
was about seven! (It has fluffy kittens
playing round the margins so I thought
you and Rainbow might like it.) But it
sounded like the dreaded pen pal letter
that you have to write for homework in
primary school so I shredded it.

There's so much tension in our house and
it's all about Darren (the pretty one,
remember?) He's the best brother in the
world but he has a serious attitude
problem right now. I don't know if it's
girlfriend trouble (make that
girlfriends trouble; he can be a bit of
a player) or exam stress but his mood
swings are worse than PMT. One minute
he's fine, the next minute he's at mum
and dad's throats.

All this crap about what he's going to do
the minute he's eighteen, and nobody can
tell him how to live his life. Juvenile
or what? I know Mum and Dad are a bit
overprotective, especially of me, but
that's just their way. We're walking on
eggshells round each other and it's not
easy. And I'm stuck in the middle of it.

Sorry to moan.
Please write back,
Caoimhe

PS Nick Lynch showed us the draft
programme for Hallowe'en when we were at
drama club on Friday night. It sounds
brill! The headline act sounds really
amazing! More on Bree's Babes, please!
(Your friend Bree?)

List time. Definitely.

1

Why headline? What headline?

2

Ring Bree at 9.01 p.m. and scream at her.

3

Devise rescue plan for B's B's.

There must be one. Mustn't there? Think outside the box, Aimée.

4

Consult the Mammy about family relationship therapy. Tonight should be timely to slip in a casual question.

Our Sunday evening ritual, conferences permitting, involves sitting together over mugs of hot chocolate to synchronise our diaries, write relevant information on the whiteboard in the kitchen and generally have a good old discussion/gossip about where our lives are at. I can't describe it without it sounding terribly formal and, well, clinical, but it's quite the opposite. It's family time, every bit as much as when the little O'Haras take their parents to McDonalds, or when Bree and Sorcha dress in waterproof protective clothing for their biannual visit to Willie's farm.

When I was little, the Da used to come round, too, and join in. Now he's more likely to be on the phone or via the latest parental toy, the webcams (his 'n' hers Christmas pressies), so we have a three-way conversation with whatever part of his head, body or the living room he has the camera pointed at. We always try to involve Rainbow, but for an extrovert moggy he's puzzlingly camera shy.

It's all a bit silly, really, given that the parents live half an hour from each other at most and come and go on an intermittent basis. But it used to make me feel really special and secure.

Still does, really.

Anyway, at these meetings, we start with the boring bits – so it was Clio's evening class schedule (unchanged), conference schedule (none this week), social schedule (salsa class, Tuesday at 8 p.m.–9.30 p.m.; parents' council, Wednesday, 8 p.m. – special topic: the twinning; meal with Jilly, Friday, 7 p.m. and both of us plan on going to Granny's on Saturday).

Rebekah and I had already been debriefed about the Firewall and Mam had read through the twinning pack so it was easy to turn the conversation to Caoimhe. And her brother. Who's been driving his family mildly potty with his moodiness.

'Caoimhe says he's been a bit moody recently and that's what I want to ask you about.'

'Does she think it's depression?'

I sensed her warming to a topic. Best nipped in the bud before it developed into an hour-long exposition.

'No, I think it's just the family dynamic, that sort of stuff –'

I didn't even get to finish. Clio launched into a veritable seminar on identity and self, the adolescent male and challenging boundaries and if I could only remember half of it, it would give me more than enough knowledge to be Caoimhe's shoulder to cry on/confidante/relationship counsellor. And maybe Darren's ... Would it have been rude to take notes?

'This is screen saver Darren Cassidy, I take it?' Clio slipped in the question with assumed nonchalance. Did I tell you she has an elephantine memory, honed to perfection through years of myopia where it is the spoken word and not the written one that delivers?

Or, as the Granny would say, there's no flies on Clio.

With the same generosity of spirit she had shown all evening, I offered to make the next hot chocolate and to let the Mammy read my email from Caoimhe.

'You must invite him here as well!' she said, reading the email.

Oh, wow! This was better than I even dared hope for. I only wanted to talk about him.

'He'll love a Derry Hallowe'en. It'll give them all a break.'

'Who?' I asked, feeling I should contribute something to the conversation.

'The family. Never underestimate the pressures of constant cohabitation on the family dynamic. You can move in with me, on the air bed, Caoimhe can have your bed and I'll ask Eamonn for a lend of his camp bed,' she went on. 'He's never used it as far as I know. He was never one for the great outdoors.'

She was at full organisational throttle. No wonder Norman-the-Head-of-Department-and-Provost-elect dotes on her.

'And once the itinerary is handed out on Wednesday at the meeting, we can plan what we'll do to fill the gaps.'

Chill out? Shop? Get to know each other better?

'I think I'll have a word with Mr and Mrs Cassidy.' Clio was unstoppable. I knew this mindset of old. 'See if you can get their email address, can you? Wait, though; you said they're older parents. You can ask Caoimhe if she thinks a letter would be better. Then I'll follow it up with a phone call. What time do they go to bed at, do you think? I wouldn't like to intrude.'

'Clio, Mammy, slow down. Whoa. Take it easy.'

'But we need to get organised. We can't leave it to Mizz whatserface, or nothing will get done. Don't quote me, Aimée, but she can be very inept. You want to see the minutes when she does them! A cross between Pitmans and Sanskrit with a nod to Ogham.'

'What's Pitmans when it's at home?'

'Shorthand. Eamonn used to have 120 words a minute. He has a certificate for it. Or maybe I have it.'

She'd got to the end of my email at this stage. 'Bree's Babes? It sounds faintly pornographic. What in God's name has that daft girl done now?'

And I told her about GoPual and the pompoms and Carly Jenkins's fallen arches and why I needed a six-week health and beauty regime and why the majorettes needed a manager and asked her what would be a good idea for a Hallowe'en costume that would be (1) original (2) tasteful or fairly tasteful and (3) flattering and before I knew it, it was half past ten and I'd forgotten all about ringing Bree and I was going to sleep on Mam's idea of going as Cleopatra.

```
From: aimeemcclogan@derry.com
To: caoimheimneverwrong@mail.net
20.12
```

```
Hi Caoimhe,
Sorry to hear your brother is having a
rough time. I hope you don't mind but I
mentioned it to my Mam - remember I told
you she's an academic-type expert on
most things pertaining to families and
relationship issues? So I hope I can
empathise with what's going on.
```

I was quite pleased with this email so far.

```
Mam insists that Darren must come to
Derry with you at Hallowe'en. She says
there's loads of room here - we have an
inflatable and a camp bed - and she'll
make sure there's lots for him to do if
```

we are busy twinning. Get him to look it
up on the web, if you haven't already.
It's the Banks of the Foyle Carnival and
it's amazing.

So I slagged it off last year. I could change my mind.

Mam wants to contact your parents. This
should be OK as she is a parent
governor, hence respectable, and has
been positively vetted. Several times.
Would a letter be best or a phone call?
And she says what time do your parents
go to bed at? So she doesn't wake them
up, I mean.

I promise to send a pic the next time.

When this latest zit epidemic has subsided and I have
lost a few pounds.

Your virtual friend,
Aimée

From: aimeemcclogan@derry.com
To: eamon.logan@mpress.com
20.40

Hi Dad,

Can't raise you on the phone so I guess
work is frantic. Can you check on

(1) your camp bed?

(2) your Bruce Springsteen's Greatest
Hits? (It is NOT for me.)

(3) your availability over Hallowe'en
when my Knockgorey twin is here?

(4) whether your paper is covering the
governors' reception for the above? If
so, try to make sure that a certain
parent governor is not interviewed
expounding on her views. A photo of her
is acceptable.

Love,
Aimée

PS See you Saturday? Before we go to
Gran's? About 3?

PPS I have been reading up on vasectomy
for my biology.

Blatant lie.

As you suggested, I see that while the
operation is reversible, fertility
cannot be guaranteed after what is
usually a safe and routine minor
procedure.

From: caoimheimneverwrong@mail.net
To: aimeemcclogan@derry.com
20.43

Thanks so much, Aimée, your Mam is
really sound. (And so are you.) Darren
has added the Derry City Council page to
his favourites and has been telling all
his mates about the Carnival. So his
mood is quite good — OK, tolerable.

What sort of a camp bed have you got?
And is the inflatable like a big airbed?
Just wondered if they'd be awkward.

And — Send. The. Pic!!

Caoimhe xx

From: aimeemcclogan@derry.com
To: caoimheimneverwrong@mail.net
21.29

Hi Caoimhe,
Thanks for the pics of you and your
Knockgorey mates. The school grounds
look huge, about twice the size of ours,
and as for the pool and fitness suite —
amazing.

Actually, Lord protect us from Castle
Grove ever getting a benefactor and a
pool and thus compulsory swimming
classes in full view of cretinous junior
school/perverts in 12V.

Shauna and Amanda sound a bit like my
BFs Rebekah and Bree. One sensible but
with hobbies/outside interests that you
don't share; and one, well, less
sensible. Matt looks cute. I take it
that's the Matt you 'like'? And the
crowd with him look good craic.

Oh, and Mam spent a night on the
inflatable bed and it's fine. Basic, but
fine. I was going to use it, give you my
bed and Darren could have the camp bed
if that's OK?

Due to an internal grievance and
artistic differences, one of the Babes
has left (Carly Jenkins's disputed
arches) and as I have taken on the
mantle of manager I have recruited
Rebekah and her sister Rachael who are
learning the routines (new sibling due
day October 10) and Bree (see attached
pic) is in charge of choreography and
costume as well as being The Lead. I
have rationalised the size of the troupe
to four, in the interests of
professionalism. (That's me in the back
row of the pic, to the left of the beech
tree. I won't be dancing. Managers
don't. It's inappropriate.)

Bigger pic to follow.
Off to rehearse the Babes,
Aimée

PS I've been talking to my Mam about the
other stuff (moods etc.). Can you ring
me? Around ten any night is good. It all
seems to be linked to testosterone and
male bits. Feel free to use the house
phone, I'm a bit low on credit on my
mobile.

Understatement. I must have owed Clio sixty quid in
top ups.

Let's not discuss this on Facebook, OK?
People are so nosy. I know all the e-
twins are on Skype, Facebook and
tweeting away already but I find it's
best to exercise caution in the face of
snooping teachers. And friends. Some
things are just personal.

Nevertheless, I went online. Just in case. To check my
emails and Facebook. Oh, looky, looky.
Breebabe was on chat.
Earthmotherbeks was on chat.

Where r u ?
Working hard?

Eighteen friends were on chat. Time for action. It's so
great to be popular.

*

Ringringring.

I checked my watch. Yes, it was after ten. This must be Caoimhe! And there was me planning on being all composed and settled in my PJs, sipping a hot chocolate, dispensing wise words ...

'Where and when can one find your mother without a search warrant and an electronic tagging device?' Not Caoimhe. Gran. And she sounded a bit miffed. 'Clio is never in.'

I didn't argue.

'I want to call over about something. And I'm not spending good money on a taxi fare until I know she's in.'

Oh? I smelled news.

'Aimée! Are you listening?'

'She should be in over most of the weekend, Gran. Day and night. Brian was an irrelevancy,' I added, in what I hoped was an offhand manner.

'Of course he was. An irrelevancy that she was being kind to. It's your mother's nature, Aimée. She attracts various waifs and strays, takes them in, counsels them, feeds them and, on one occasion, married one! You worry too much about your parents, Aimée,' she added more gently. 'They can look after themselves now, you know. Well, maybe not that well in your father's case ...'

'Gran!'

'Well, you know what I mean. I saw him in the town the other day apprehending people in the street. Again.'

'It's called doing vox pops, Gran. It's his job.'

'Like I said, stopping random people outside Tesco and asking them personal questions about the government. I could have told him a thing or two but he didn't stop me. The older generation is invisible, Aimée. Invisible. You'll find that out if you are spared to your eighties. Then you'll understand why my meditation mantra is "Nobody tramps on my dahlias." It's so much more empowering than all that letting-yourself-float-into-the-light nonsense. Life's too short and precious to be ground underfoot.'

A full scale geriatric rant?

'They only come looking for your opinion if they want you as a guinea pig for some sort of intergenerational, cross-border, cross-community, EU-funded –'

'Hold it, Gran. I think I know what this is about. Is it an invite to a focus group meeting? The twinning committee asked the governors to draw up proposals for elderly inclusion. I know Mam was putting your name down for the focus group.'

'What?'

'The school want to involve the Third Age in the whole twinning process. I know they're working on some sort of intergenerational social history scrapbook thing. Twinning over-fifty-five-year-olds with Year 12s. Clio probably put your name forward.'

'I had worked that out for myself, Aimée. That is why I was looking for her. When you see your mother, please inform her that if people over fifty-five are now classed as elderly, her time is running out. Fast.'

'But Gran ... you will take part?'

'I will not be some sort of social experiment for a bunch of students. It's ... well, it's disrespectful. And I'm sure we won't get paid. What do people think pensioners live on? Certainly not their pension.'

'But Gran, it'd be a real shame if you don't take part. You have so many great stories to share.' Flattery, the last resort of the desperate.

'That is quite true, but please remind your mother that I am already committed to the themed t'ai chi demonstration in the Guildhall Square before the carnival parade and it takes a lot of rehearsal. Some of those taking part, quite frankly, are a bit past it. And there are our costumes to make. Not all of us oldies have endless time on our hands, you know.'

What costumes, pray? Spare me.

'Mind you,' she went on, and I detected a senior citizen warming to her favourite topic, 'you have a point. There can't be many people round here who drove a fire engine in the Blitz.'

And she is not one of those people. Unless Hitler held off invading Poland until she was old enough to get her driving licence. But it's true that my gran has had an eventful life. And, like Clio, once she gets started on a topic, there's no stopping her.

Thank goodness it isn't hereditary.

Chapter Seven

ell, of course I couldn't *not* share all this with Caoimhe, could I? I won't bore you with all the trivia of our exchanges, but suffice to say that over the previous week or so she had become fully conversant with the vagaries of my dysfunctional family. It was only fair, really, as it meant when she came to stay at Riverview, she'd be fully briefed on the domestic situation. And I expect she was passing it all on to Darren. I'd stressed to her how important that was.

But she seemed to find said vagaries 'endearing' (not my adjective of choice but infinitely preferable to the epithet – 'colourful' – that those in authority tended to attach to the McCourt-Logans, as a more polite synonym for 'odd'). And I hesitate to say this. But she is a lot less self-absorbed than my BFs here. I know Rebekah was poised to be an active birthing partner or whatever for Mrs O'H and Bree's mental, physical and emotional energy was devoted to GoPual and Planet Lurrrrrve. (At fifteen. Sad.) I understood that. I wasn't being disloyal. I'm only saying …

Caoimhe's really good about replying too. If I have one teeny complaint it's that she could be a bit more forthcoming about Darren. I mean, I need to build up a mental profile to match his photo. Looks aren't everything, after all. She's told me lots about Knockgorey and her drama class and her girlfriends – but not a lot about her social life. With a brother like Darren, she's bound to have one. I mean, all his friends must be hanging round their house. She never says much about going up the town, either. I know she hardly ever goes into Dublin cos it's (a) expensive, (b) too adult an environment for her to be out in and (c) a bit dangerous in places but maybe if/when I go to stay with her I can work on her parents a bit. Clio reminds me that I've grown up with a lot more freedom to make my own choices than most fifteen-year-olds because of her and Eamonn's parental policy of Controlled Neglect. And Caoimhe's far too chatty and pretty and lively to be a social misfit. Isn't she?

*

Eleven o'clock already. I'd better turn in. I'll just check my messages. No, nothing new from Caoimhe. A quick look at Facebook? Two messages from Beks, three from

Bree, one from Carly Jenkins, one from Simon C-K on chat (did I accept him as a friend? Must have. Why?). It's all just the usual stuff, wanting to know where I am, that kind of thing.

I must charge my phone overnight. I look at it. Five missed calls. Five! Stalkers? And texts – there are a LOT of them. From Saturday. And Friday night. Oops. Surely we talked at school on Friday? I had that meeting of the twinning committee and it went on for ever. Thursday night? Wednesday, 07.10 a.m.? This is strange. I mean, I've been chatting away to Caoimhe. We've got so much to sort out in such a short time. I'm busy. Don't the girls realise it's getting really close to Hallowe'en? I had my phone on silent when I was on the computer. It's no good if you keep getting interrupted by random calls, is it? I mean, this twinning is for all of us.

From Bree:

> Need to talk ASAP. Where are you? Have u got cozzies sorted?

Then Beks:

> Need to get cozzies sorted asap. Ring/email/text/Facebook— anything!!

I suppose it's my own fault for organising them for years. No self-motivation.

Another from Bree:

> WTF RU? Trying u all wkend. All OK? PS Beks looking 4 u 2.

And as I read, the screen lights up:

> U OK? CU 2moro x Beks.

I ought to text back but if I do she'll start up a conversation and I'm knackered. I'll catch her in the morning. Could there be a touch of envy that she and Bree don't have a new Facebook friend?

*

'It's not like you. That's all I'm saying. You're usually so organised.' Rebekah paced the touchline like the expectant sister she is.

I misinterpreted her. Wilfully. I knew it was a dig about the (lack of) Hallowe'en costumes but I took it as a derogation of my managerial skills for Bree's Babes.

'Well, I think we've made great progress. The troupe may be small in number but it's dynamic. Now. One more time.'

I pressed the button. 'Born in the USA' blared out and Rebekah ran to take her place behind Bree in the line-up, muttering, 'You know very well that's not what I mean.'

'C'mon, girls. Kick!'

Bree has put an advertisement on the school notice-board and in the local free paper. 'Bree's Babes: Majorettes for Hire – no stadium too big, no sporting occasion too small,' followed by my mobile number. A blatant disregard for Eamonn's views on freesheets being delivered door-to-door by exploited immigrant senior citizens, proselytism, a living wage for unionised journos, etc., etc., etc.

And it is patently a lie and contravention of the Trades Descriptions Act. I mean, if you put the four of them in Croke Park or Lansdowne Road they'd look like a small but disciplined fringe protest. Still, with Carly pushed sideways to assistant choreographer/dresser and Rebekah and her next-sequential sisters Hannah (thirteen and a half) and Rachael (eleven) replacing Carly and Patricia Wannabe, albeit on a diminutive sample scale, the routine is one of the stronger parts of Castle Grove's Carnival. Don't dwell too long on what that says about the rest of the programme.

Across the pitch, on the tennis courts, a crowd of 12R and 12O was helping Mr MacDonnell with his joints or hospital corners or whatever it was that was crucial to the Shared Heritage float. I know that, as Clio's daughter, I should have checked what percentage of his workforce is female but I couldn't summon up the enthusiasm. 12V and E, Mizz Hardy instructed crisply this morning, are to be removed from the ranks of the chainsawers and power drillers and tasked with painting the canvas backdrop with images depicting the life of Colmcille. Health and safety regulations, and rightly so. Inclusion is no excuse for distributing weapons of mass destruction.

Gran's t'ai chi dance, as demonstrated in her kitchen on Saturday, was (I have to admit) impressive, and that was only the scaled-down version. Her fellow exponents are drawing on a total of several centuries' experience in the shirt industry to craft capes representing the four elements. (She's fire, naturally – oranges and warm reds are her colour palette.) Their soundtrack, which I transferred onto her iPod for her, is an interesting mix of the lavatory music at the Mandarin Garden and whales communicating underwater, which presumably creates the desired ambience to transport the crowd far from a wet and windy autumn evening in Derry.

The cross-generational scrapbook exhibition is on the proverbial long finger and the school input to the general fancy dress parade is, according to Mizz H, 'ad hoc, disparate, free structure'. Which means nobody has a clue what anyone else is going as unless they are actually on the float, but that ninety-nine per cent of the boys will be in skirts, full make-up, stilettos and suspenders. Nothing new there, then.

My nonchalance about this is unusual. But frankly, I have more on my mind. And I know I was snappy with Clio when she hovered round the bedroom door last night proffering a black wig and a length of gold brocade.

This year, for the first time since, what, Primary Five? it is Not My Problem.

Thus far, I have lost a miserable total of one and a half pounds which, as Bree pointed out, represents a big pee. My zits have been playing join-the-dots until my nose and T-zone area looks like one gigantic pus ball, and the haircut and new jeans are on indefinite hold.

The camp bed is *in situ*, ready for assembly; a new duvet and covers have been ordered; Gran, Clio and I filled the freezer last Sunday and the only part of the host home which is unprepared is the hostess. But I still have eleven days.

Even the governors had no difficulty with Clio inviting Darren. Inclusion. How could they object?

And Clio says Mr and Mrs Cassidy sound lovely and not geriatric at all. They just don't do email. Or disaffected teenagers. I hope they don't decide to hop on an Aer Arann Happy Hour special and pay a surprise visit to 1A Riverview.

'You are just not with us these days,' Rebekah observed wryly, and I realised the pompoms were packed away and it was time to go. 'Are you spending long hours at your PC surfing for costume designs or are you lusting over your screen saver? No, Aimée,' she interrupted my protest, 'do not even think of denying it. And,' she added, with uncharacteristic meanness, 'we all know that you somehow connived to have Darren Cassidy sleeping under your roof when he shouldn't even be on the exchange trip.'

'But Clio insisted –'

'Sometimes,' Rebekah said through pursed lips, 'Clio is too inclusive for her own good.

'And the fact that you have not issued me with a poly pocket of printed instructions about Hallowe'en means that you are keeping your options open and that Darren – oh, and Caoimhe of course, mustn't forget her – well, that they feature large in your imagination.'

Again, she stopped my attempt at self-justification. 'Aimée Logan,' she reproved me, 'I have known you most of your life and you do not do spontaneous. Ever.'

'I'm sorry,' I told her as she shepherded Rachael and Hannah towards the bus stop. 'I did know what you meant. It's just … I want to be a really good hostess – oh OK then, of course I fancy him – who wouldn't? And you do not need to spread that piece of information –'

'Correct, friend. Your face and body language will do it for you.'

'I know I need to sort out our costumes. But I have been busy. We all have, thanks to this Babes carry-on. I'll get started tonight. And of course, we'll all be going together, the three of us, once we pick a theme.' I stopped short, seeing her face.

'Well, that's just it. You see, I'm thinking of going on the float. Instead.'

Rebekah doesn't 'think of'. She does. So that meant she *was* going on the float. Was that what this verbal attack, this attempt at character assassination, had been about? Was she trying to defend her indefensible decision?

'Tom's been chosen as one of the Columban Fathers,' she rushed on. 'It's quite prestigious, really, it's not just positive discrimination because he's down as "any other faith or tradition or none" on the equality monitoring forms. He's asked me to take part in the pageant, too, as one of the Celtic maidens.' Crucial punchline delivered, she rabbited on. 'It's really simple. The art and design department are running up a pile of dark green skirts with elasticated waists – you know, one size fits all – and they're making big cloaks, so all we have to do is turn up wearing our white short-sleeved shirts and our pumps. But they need people they can depend on to turn up on the night. Not people who'll disappear up the town or go on the piss. Tom says I'd be very good,' she continued apologetically, 'because I'm so reliable.'

'So you are.' I sounded wounded, I knew.

Judas.

'And what about Bree?' I sneered. 'Is she swelling the ranks of comely maidens at the crossroads?'

'What are you on about?'

'Is she on Tom's float?' I didn't mean to roar at her. Honestly.

'Don't be silly, Aimée. And it's not Tom's float. He's just one of the few 12R students who's committed to it.'

We walked on in silence for a few yards.

'Bree says she was trying to get you last night. And the night before,' Rebekah continued.

I felt her eyes on my face, watching for reaction.

'She said she couldn't get through on the phone. Or your mobile. She tried for ages. Then she asked me to try in case there was a fault. Then we thought maybe you had it off the hook. Both nights. And you never replied to my messages on Facebook.'

Rebekah is far from stupid.

'For two or three nights? That's hardly disappearing off the face of the earth.'

'It is for you. What's it with the Cassidys that we can't all join in? Aimée, Darren Cassidy's a player. His own sister said so. What are you going to do when he gets here? Insist 12G wear burqas? Not that you don't look ...' Her voice trailed off. She knew she had said way too much. 'Bree asked me to pass you a message before she went off in a hurry to meet Paul off the bus back from the 8K inter-colleges,' she stumbled on. 'Look, don't shoot the messenger, right?'

And it all came rushing out. 'She said to tell you they've decided what they're doing and they're all going as gangsters. There's a whole crowd of them. Carly and Brendan and Infectious Mickey and – Aimée, don't throw a hissy fit. It doesn't suit you ...'

'True to type,' I sniffed. And I only just stopped myself from adding 'for the Sycamore Heights crowd'. That would have been bitchy and cheap. True, but cheap.

'Sorcha's helping them with the costumes,' Rebekah prattled on. 'Bree and the girls are going as molls. Well, sexy gangsters.'

'And what does a sexy gangster wear?'

'Not a lot, probably,' Rebekah answered truthfully.

'And what if this great romance doesn't make it to Hallowe'en?'

'It's been three months now. Almost.' Rebekah had clearly thought this through. 'Look, Aimée, I don't see the big attraction any more than you do but Paul is her choice and we've got to respect the fact that she's serious about him.'

'Bree! Serious?!'

'Yes. She *is*. Come on, Aimée, she doesn't even *like* Carly Jenkins that much, she only hangs about with her now because she's going with Paul's mate Brendy ...'

I felt dizzy. My peer group was dissolving around me.

'And when did you plan all this with Tom? Surely not at the Firewall? When you were ...' (I made speech marks with my fingers) "keeping an eye on Griffin"?'

'Aim-ee! Don't be like that. That was weeks ago.'

'So you've been meeting him since then?'

'Not like that. Not like Bree and Paul.'

'But you're always so busy,' I argued. 'You never have time –'

'Not *never*. Just not often. And like I said, it's not like that. Can you see us trying to gatecrash Jaguar? Get real, Aimée. Tom's a really nice person, y'know. And he has his own stuff to deal with.'

Us. She said *us*. Us is me and Rebekah and Bree. Not Rebekah and Tom and the cast of Colmcille's Journey.

Not Bree and GoPual and Carly and Brendy and the human detritus from the underclass that is Sycamore Heights. What was happening in my life?

Rebekah took my stunned silence for disapproval. Which, in a way, it was.

'Come on, Aimée. So maybe I haven't been telling you everything that happens in my life. But I'm not the only one who's holding out. At least Tom's here.'

I swivelled round.

'Not here right now. But he's not like somebody you've only met online or talked to on the phone. They are who they say they are, or who you think they are. I *know* Tom. And Tom will still be here, in Derry, when the exchange visit is done and dusted. I'm sorry if that sounds bitchy,' she called over her shoulder as she followed her sisters up the steps on to the bus, 'but it's true. You told us you were making new friends for us all. You were supposed to be networking. No way. Think about it, Aimée. It's not *like* you to be so out of touch with your real friends. Just think about it.'

*

That was exactly what the Mammy found me doing when she came back salsa-ed out: thinking about it.

We exchanged pleasantries, trivia. She offered coffee. I declined. I offered cookies. She looked surprised. (After three weeks' manic calorie counting, whining and complaining from her daughter, she had every right to be.) She declined.

'I was going to see what we could make out of that gold brocade,' Clio ventured after a few more inconsequential exchanges, 'but you were never off your computer last night. Or Sunday night, either. And your mobile's off so I take it you've used up all your credit.' Pause. 'So I assume you're all sorted?' she went on. 'It's not a problem. I wasn't interfering or anything. I just thought you two would look good as Cleopatra and Charmian. You know, Rebekah with her dark colouring and ... and I showed you Jilly's wig. She doesn't want it back so we can cut away at it. I thought maybe Sorcha would help me run up the costumes, if Bree was involved, too ... but then I expect she's dressing up along with Paul.'

What? This was my own mother talking. Another Judas.

'Come on, love, she's been going out with him for ... how long? Three or four months? Since the summer, anyway. It's hardly a shock.' So my face had betrayed me, too. 'That's unheard of for Bree. It's unheard of for her mother, come to that. So it must be serious. Silly girl that she is,' she added quickly. 'And couples who are going steady usually dress up to complement each other. Don't they? You know, Bonnie and Clyde, Romeo and Juliet. It's what you do. It's tradition.'

Never in my short life had I seen a Shakespearean couple grace the Banks of the Foyle parade and nor do I ever expect to do so. But it's what people 'do'. Apparently.

'And how is Rebekah? She hasn't been round for a few days,' Clio probed, more gently. 'I take it she's going with you?'

'She's going on the float. With Tom. Tom Harrison. As an Irish girl. That's dead simple.'

Mammy ignored the sarcasm.

'Tom Harrison? I know his mother. Well, I know *of* her. Friends of friends and all that. I didn't know he and Rebekah –'

'They're not.'

'I see. So …'

'Yes, Mam, so. So I have no one to go out with at Hallowe'en and no hope of looking the way I want to look by then, either. In or out of costume.'

'We must go up the town on Saturday and get those jeans,' she suggested.

'No.' I shake my head. 'I'm not getting them in the same size that I already have. There's no point in throwing away money. Wait till the ten fits.'

Tears pricked my eyes. I blinked. Why was I nearly crying?

Clio moved in to hug me. To my surprise, I let her.

'I wish we could see into the future,' Clio mused, 'because I know you won't believe me when I tell you that so much will change in these next few years. Take Bree, for example. I reckon she's peaked early.'

'She's what?'

'Peaked early. It happens all the time,' Clio assured me. 'Yesterday's skinny child is today's gamine waif is tomorrow's full blown rose. Or mutton dressed as Primark lamb.'

'Like Sorcha?' I ventured.

'I didn't say that.' Clio pursed her lips in mock disapproval. 'But I promise you, Aimée, no one gets away with a diet of junk food and unhealthy choices for ever.'

OK, Clio. So vengeance will be mine in my menopausal years. Personally, I'd settle for the here and now.

'But,' she continued forcefully, 'there's the other issue here. You can't expect to go on running other people's lives for ever, Aimée.'

What?

'I mean, you're a brilliant organiser,' she went on. 'It's one of your strengths. Just like you have great intuition. Most of the time. Like the way you picked up on Caoimhe not wanting to sleep on a camp bed, though goodness knows why; she doesn't sound pretentious. I'm a bit like that, too. Eamonn isn't. He's quite the opposite. But some people like being disorganised. They might call it spontaneous. I know,' she adds comfortingly, 'it doesn't sit easily with me, either. But in a couple of months, you'll all be sixteen.'

Was this a sermon?

'I can hardly believe it. I'm sure Sorcha and Mrs O'Hara can't believe it either. But you're all starting to want to work out things for yourselves, Aimée. To go your own ways. That doesn't mean friendships end.' She looked directly into my eyes. 'But they change. They adapt. If we're lucky, sometimes they grow. Now,' she added, breaking free and heading for the kettle, 'that is quite enough counselling for this week.'

'For this year,' I tried to joke. I smiled weakly. 'Mam, do you really think I try to run other people's lives for them?'

'Well, what about your dad and Fiona?' she asked gently. 'Or you and Gran interrogating me about poor Brian? That's going beyond filial concern, I think.'

The kettle shrilled into action.

'I must get on with this essay,' Clio concluded, refilling her mug. 'Give me a shout later, after you've had your marathon chat with Caoimhe, will you? And you know, Rebekah, for one, might be glad to hear a little more about what's going on there, too. Bring her into the chat. We all get paranoid if we feel left out.'

From: aimeemcclogan@derry.com
To: caoimheimneverwrong@mail.net
20.49

Hi Caoimhe,
Ring me at ten, as planned. On the house phone.

If Darren's lurking, email me and we'll reschedule. Or text but I can't tb - I really can't tap Clio for more phone credit. I've just had a big heart-to-heart with her about friendship, secrets and independence. I can see why she's so good at her job!

And could you talk to my BFs on Facebook chat? I know what the schools said but everyone's doing it, we both know that. And I reckon Rebekah is seriously miffed and feels left out - but don't say I said that.

Talk 18r,
Aimée x

Chapter
Eight

From: caoimheimneverwrong@mail.net
To: aimeemcclogan@derry.com
21.09

Hi Aimée,
Sorry for the delay. Darren was a pain
all last night and he and Dad had a real
shouting match, which is unheard of (for
Dad). Dad had a go at him about only
wanting to go to Derry to 'run the
streets'. He said all the stuff about
Darren wanting to look out for me and to
suss out the Magee campus was a 'pack of
lies'. That's strong language for Dad.

Then brother dear stomped off to see his
latest sort-of girlfriend, Caryn, and
she went all possessive about the Derry
trip which was a Big Mistake. So she's
now his ex sort-of girlfriend. And then
he moans to me about how nobody
understands him etc. etc. etc. He says
he wants to access my Facebook page so
he can talk to your friends! Can't
imagine why! Lol.

I've friended Bree and Rebekah on
Facebook. I can't wait to meet them
online - it's a shame neither of them
has brothers!!! He's great but he'd wear
you down,

Stuck in the middle,
Caoimhe x

Darren wants to chat with Bree and Rebekah on
Facebook, and Caoimhe can't imagine why. LOL.

Clearly he wasn't attracted to the sliver of me he saw
peeping out from behind a tree in the school pic. But
maybe he wasn't not-attracted, either. Sort of neutral.
Ambivalent?

This could be my chance to show off my cerebral
strengths and ready caustic wit, my *joie de vivre* and
dynamic personality. What do you reckon, Rainbow?

MMMwwmmurr.

I thought as much. Thank you, Rainbow. So this is a
chance for my witty repartee and cogent yet incisive

thought process to shine out like a good deed in a naughty world, as Gran would say?

Weeaoww.

Would that it were my photo that was arousing his interest! No, censor that superficial, shallow, sexist thought. Right now.

*

At one minute past ten, the phone rang. I snatched up the receiver.

'Hey,' said Caoimhe.

'Hiya.'

'Right. Can you stay on the phone until I come up on Facebook? Are the girls on, d'you know?'

'Is Darren with you?' I feigned nonchalance. Badly.

'Not right now but he is really made up about coming, y'know. He can't wait. Specially now he's single again, he says.'

Chill, Aimée, take things at face value. Why wouldn't Darren be excited about coming to Derry for Hallowe'en? Derry *is* Hallowe'en. I would not – I repeat, *not* – allow myself to lurch between vain hope that he wants to meet me and the near certainty that he (a) fancies Bree, (b) is a player and (c) might just have enough charisma to blow out GoPual. While I end up as his asexual and platonic confidante, counsellor and tour guide. A virtual sister. I do not want to be a virtual sister. I don't want to be the reliable female friend – which is the only thing I seem to be to the male population of Castle Grove.

So could he be interested? Even playing hard to get? Further speculation was too much for a nearly-sixteen-year-old whose psychoanalytic skills have only been tested on a cat.

As soon as Caoimhe was online I hung up and rang Rebekah.

'Hi, stranger.'

'Less of that. Come up on Facebook. Caoimhe's on. Bye.'

And Beks duly appeared.

> Hiya. Mum having some sort of contractions so am on standby. Wot's t craic n Dublin?

And so it continued, and it was great the way we all interacted. Not deep and meaningful but just nice and relaxed. Like we'd known each other for ages and not just a matter of weeks. Bree failed to materialise. Well ... I failed to ring her.

*

The Facebook three-way was, of course, on the agenda for discussion when Beks came home with me after school the next day. She made the opening gambit. 'About this Darren crisis –' she began.

'What Darren crisis?' I asked.

'Come on, Aimée. Caoimhe was being as discreet as she could but it was clear from last night that there has been some kind of row in the Cassidy household and it seems to centre on the trip to Derry.'

'Yeah?' I muttered. 'That's hardly a crisis.'

'Exactly. But you are turning it into one.'

'Why would I do that?'

'Well ... oh, Aimée. Maybe it suits you, you know?

You like … managing people. And because you fancy him – yes, you do – that's one reason why you are … making something out of nothing. I think all that happened was that Caoimhe had a bad day at home – we all do – and she poured her heart out to you because she had no one to talk to. And you were miles away. And a stranger,' Beks added, unhelpfully. Then, catching my eye, 'I don't mean it was just because you were a stranger. She must have known you'd be … kind. But Caoimhe would know it didn't matter if you gossiped as you're in a different part of the country – not that you do gossip, Aimée …'

'Thanks,' I muttered, as she stopped short before she dug an even deeper hole for herself.

'Look, Caoimhe told you about a row at home. So what? All families have bad days – well, maybe not you and Clio, Aimée, but all *normal* families, if you know what I mean,' Rebekah pressed on. 'I think you're deter-mined to dramatise the whole thing – you know, setting yourself up as a listening ear for a lad who probably just wants out on the town to eye up the talent. He's seven-teen, Aimée,' she added, more kindly. 'Seventeen and single and far from home – when he gets here, like. He'll be a player. They all are. Well, most of them.'

'I am not setting myself up –' I stopped short. This is my best friend who reads me like … like Clio can.

'I don't want you getting let down,' Beks said quietly. 'I reckon this is your need to be needed coming out, Aimée. Maybe Darren doesn't want sympathy. Maybe he just wants attention. You don't have to solve other people's problems, you know. You can end up being used. You *can*,' she insisted. 'You need to have more self-esteem.'

'Yeah.'

'You know what I mean.' Beks squeezed my arm. 'If he has a fling with some serial maneater like Patricia Wannabe or some of her crowd, it's his loss. It'll just show you're too good for him,' she added, so loyally I felt a lump in my throat. 'You could do a lot better, Aimée, than some over-dramatic Dub who loves himself!'

'What makes you think he's like that?' I asked.

'OK, so I'm reading between the lines,' Rebekah admitted. 'But ... Dubs are notoriously over-dramatic. Everyone says so. Be sure you don't sell yourself short. And say nothing to Bree,' she added. 'Not that she'd notice right now.'

'Do you think she minded not being in on things last night?' I asked tentatively. 'Maybe I should have rung her.'

'I already had. She was out with Paul. Incommunicado. No contest.' Rebekah grinned.

And we both laughed. Together. For the first time in two days.

*

In an attempt to recreate old times, Clio had laid on a huge pot of veggie curry and made poppadoms and was hovering at a discreet distance. She'd even got Rainbow offside by the blatant bribery of letting him sleep on her fluffy cushions, which are usually out of (feline) bounds.

'You're not sore about Tom?' Beks chanced, as we crumbled the final poppadom between us. (Gran says if you eat the last one of anything on a plate you risk being an old maid. No point in tempting fate.)

'No. Not now. I was surprised, I suppose.'

'Why?'

'Because it's always Bree who runs after blokes – no, no, I know you didn't run after him, jeez, because you never bother about having a boyfriend, you're always too busy and because we laugh at all the stupid eejits in our year at school.'

'Tom's not a stupid eejit.'

'I didn't mean that. Of course he's not. And I'm not intimidating, either.'

She laughed.

Then Scary Bree turned up.

'This curry is delicious, Clio. Like old times, really.'

Old times? Old? We are not yet sixteen and we are reminiscing. How sad is that?

Clio virtually blushed with pleasure and went into earth-mother mode, offering to whip up the macrobiotic contents of our fridge into Something Delicious for Dessert.

'I'm really glad you invited me round,' Bree continued, shovelling down a second helping, 'cause I wanted to ask your advice, Clio.'

What was going on? How come Clio had asked her over? What the …? I sensed plotting behind my back.

'It's about Men Who Won't Commit,' Bree confided between mouthfuls of aloo gobi. 'I know you're an authority …'

Amazingly, Clio fell for this unashamed cheesing and by the time we'd started on the second tub of Ben and Jerry's Chocolate Macadamia (with home-made yoghurt and organic apricot sauce), GoPual had been elevated to the status of core topic for a post-feminist workshop. With personal details changed to protect the hapless, of course. It'll probably be the pinnacle of his academic career and he won't even know.

Ringringring.

It was Rebekah's phone.

She walked towards the window to get a better signal, her face animated.

'I'm on my way!' she squealed and immediately rang off and dialled a taxi for Altnagelvin hospital. Mrs O'H, it seemed, was already en route in an ambulance and Mr O'H had, as predicted, opted to mind the flock while Beks went to the labour ward. It smacks of role reversal – that's why Clio was so enthused by it.

'The younger ones won't feel excluded or marginalised, and they and their daddy can welcome the new arrival together, as a corporate familial group.'

Boll-*ocks* – Mr O'Hara just can't stand the sight of blood. Or the sound of screaming women.

As we clucked out the door together to wait for the taxi, Bree cast her eyes heavenwards. 'Excuse me!' – her mobile was ringing – 'Beks, wait! Can I share your taxi? It won't take you far out of your way to go past Sycamore Heights, your mum will be pushing for hours yet. Beks ... Beks, please ... wait for me ... oh, all right then ...'

I closed the door on matters maternal. For now.

To do

1
Thank Clio for curry.

2
Find New Baby (sex unspecific) card and lemon sleepsuit (a misnomer, no doubt), 0-3 months, bought three weeks ago for infant O'Hara in case of premature arrival.

3
Feed Rainbow, who is gnawing ravenously at the cords of my dressing gown in a frenzy of night starvation.

4
But first, another brownie ...

Chapter
Nine

*L*ater, I noticed that Caoimhe had sent me two
email messages. Two?

From: caoimheimneverwrong@mail.net
To: aimeemcclogan@derry.com
21.24

Thanks again for lending an ear. Shauna
and Amanda are great but I can't talk to

them about the Darren thing because it's
all too close to home and it would get
straight back to Mum and Dad. They'd
think I was 'mouthing'. But then if you
were at Knockgorey I couldn't talk to
you either, I suppose, so the twinning
must be fate.

Also, Darren suggested phoning/chatting
with you and your friends, you know, as
a way for things not to be so awkward
when he comes with me to Castle Grove.
Hope you don't mind me passing him your
number and I hope you and Darren hit it
off! I can never be cross with him for
long. Like I told you on the phone, he
always stood up for me when I got
bullied at our last school.

Anyway, NO MORE MOANING!!

About the costumes — I'll fit in with
whatever you and your mum come up with.
Let me know what I owe you,

Caoimhe x

PS Beks will make an amazing child
psychiatrist.

She is so right. Be still my hormones. I clicked the latest
email.

```
From: caoimheimneverwrong@mail.net
To: aimeemcclogan@derry.com
21.42

Hi Aimée,
10 p.m. suit? I'll ring you.
Darren

(via Caoimhe's email)
```

'Darren's ringing me in a minute,' I informed the Mammy.

She appeared unfazed.

'So ... what should I say to him, you know, I mean, will I tell him a bit more about Castle Grove?'

'Since when have you been at a loss for words?' Clio sounded exasperated. Then, more kindly, she added, 'Look, love, he's coming here as our guest. The worst that can happen is that he turns out to be a total freeloader. If he gets into any bother – and I do not think for one minute that he will – he's answerable to his parents and his school and the whole twinning project as well as to us. I do tutor students not much older than him, you know. I'm sure I can handle one more adolescent male. Don't be building this up into something it's not,' she counselled. 'And don't agree to anything you're not happy about,' she added, as an afterthought.

Like what, mother?

I took the precaution of minimising the screen on my PC and made a mental note to change my screen saver. Looking into his eyes while talking with him over the phone would be too disconcerting. Him looking into my eyes in my bedroom would be too embarrassing.

The phone rang. That'd be him.

'Hi, Aimée? How's it going?'

Warm. Cheery. And I have always been a sucker for a voice like an RTÉ newscaster.

'I'm really nervous about ringing you, you know.'

And he sounded it. *Not.*

'I just don't want to say the wrong thing and mess it all up for Caoimhe. I can be a bit tactless sometimes. And she's so looking forward to going up to Derry. So am I.'

Totally disarmed already, I managed an (empathic?) 'Mmm.'

'Your mum seems really sound. Mine's a bit more –'

'Conventional?' I offered.

'I was going to say narrow-minded. But I think the word is conventional, yes. Traditional. And older than your mum.'

'Clio's not as young as she acts,' I interjected treacherously.

'So. Tell you what. Caoimhe says I can go on her Facebook page and chat as long as I say straight away who I am. Just this once. Could we add in your friends as well? That'd be so good.'

Whaaat? They're *my* girlfriends, not his. Not even potentially.

He took my gobsmacked silence for stupidity. This was not part of my plan.

'You know, the girls you're always chatting to Caoimhe about. There's the one that calls herself the earth mother – that's Rebekah, right? And the dancer. Bree. Could you set that up for us? I really want –'

'It depends on what they're doing. They're very busy people.'

Caoimhe was supposed to chat on to Darren about *me*, not my mates.

'Rebekah's mum has just gone into labour, so she's kind of tied up with family stuff. I'm sure Caoimhe's told you that. And Bree –' I could not bring myself to think of her as 'the dancer' – 'Bree's always with her boyfriend so she may not be about. It's *serious*.'

'Jesus! I mean, she's fifteen – and she's a real looker, isn't she?'

I did not want to hear this.

'Oh, they're *very* serious,' I insisted. 'They've been going steady for ages now.' It wasn't really a lie. I mean, define 'ages' in a teen relationship? 'So Bree's not likely to be about,' I stressed.

What did I sound like? Were those clipped, censorious tones really mine?

'Hey, chill, Aimée, I only asked … I just thought it'd be good, y'know … OK, not tonight, but you could set it up, soon. I mean, we'll be up in Derry in ten days. What's your problem?'

Don't you have any cop-on, Darren?

'I'm sorry,' I said tersely, 'but I'm not responsible for how my girlfriends live their lives. I didn't realise it was so important to you,' I snapped sarcastically.

There was a long pause. Was he still there? What had I done? Had I come across as paranoid?

'Can we start again, seeing as we're going to be spending two days together very soon?'

I could feel the warmth of the smile in his voice. Smug bastard. He'd guessed. Damn him.

Act cool. Calm your hormones, Aimée. It's no big deal. Remember, this boy is using you – isn't he?

Only if you let yourself be used, a little voice said. It went unheeded.

I really need to do spontaneous now and then. Don't I? I'm too young to be boring and predictable. As well as gullible and bitchy.

'Aimée? Are you still there? Don't hang up on me. Please.'

As if I would have. Function, mouth. *Now*.

'I've no intention of hanging up. It's not my style. To be honest, I've spent a fair bit of today clearing the air with my mother and with Bree and Beks. So maybe it's time I did the same with you.'

Who said that? Me, as in Aimée? Assertive, or what?

'I just want to make it clear that I'm not going to be a conduit' I rate that word 'for setting you up with any of my very good friends who might just happen to have seen your picture and –'

Pause. Breathe, Aimée. Or alter-ego-Aimée.

'– and be interested in what they may interpret as new talent. Talent that will be disappearing back to Dublin the minute Santa's grotto appears in the shopping centres.' (Traditionally, that's November 1st.) 'I don't mean Bree, of course,' alter-ego-Aimée rushed on, 'like I said, she's spoken for. And Beks is far too busy at the moment. But there are … others. I think I should make that clear,' I concluded with a gulp. 'And,' I added, against my better judgement, 'I should make it clear that Bree is not a trained dancer. Far from it.'

'She's got great legs, though.'

I didn't rise to this. I only sent a head and shoulders photo – didn't I? And even that was mostly tree.

Another silence. Over to you, Darren. I could wait.

He whistled down the phone in an affected manner. Drama queen.

'So … I see. My little sister has told you I'm a player? And put the frighteners on the Derry virgins? Right.'

'Derry virgins is a contradiction in terms,' I muttered before I could stop myself.

'An oxymoron, like,' he laughed.

RTÉ accent. Literate. Sense of humour. Kind enough to laugh at a tired joke. I was lost.

Help me, Rainbow.

'I really am looking forward to coming to Derry, Aimée. It looks magic. I'm never off the website.'

'So why don't you have your own Facebook page? If you use the Internet so much?'

A pause, then I heard the laughter in his voice.

'*Touché*, Aimée. I should, I know. I'm just too idle, I guess. And Caoimhe's the Internet guru in our house. She spends so much time on it. Obviously. It's great for her.'

Obviously, should it not be great for him too?

'I'll get her to sort it for me,' he added, much too glibly.

'It's not difficult,' I told him.

'I just never felt the need before,' he replied. 'Usually I talk to most of my mates face to face, every day.'

And now? You may make friends far from Foxrock? No, Aimée, lighten up.

And so we exchanged trivia about the carnival, the floats, school, whatever, and he was really, really easy to chat to. Just like Caoimhe. No, easier than Caoimhe. More laid back. More confident.

But other times, he sounded like he wasn't. Typical bloke, then.

Suddenly, it was half past ten and, reluctantly, we agreed it was time to hang up.

Clio looked happier.

'You're sorted? It's not too late, Aimée, you know that. If you're not happy about Darren coming –'

'It's fine,' I interjected, probably too enthusiastically.

'Your dad's coming over on Friday. He wants to talk about what you could do when your guests are here. He thought they might like a tour of the office or a drive into Donegal if it's nice.'

'He doesn't have a girlfriend. Not a real one, anyway.'

Clio looked puzzled.

'What? You mean he and Fiona –'

'Darren. Darren doesn't have a real girlfriend.'

Mothers can be dense sometimes, They should pay better attention to their offspring's news. Thus do rumours originate.

```
From: aimeemcclogan@derry.com
To:caoimheimneverwrong@mail.net
23.02

Hi Caoimhe,
It was good to talk to Darren. He's
really sound. Like you said.
```

Too much? No?

```
I'm sure he's told you all about our
chat.


I'm really looking forward to
Hallowe'en!
```

Maybe we can use Facebook chat before
then, so my Derry muckers can join in
again. (Hope you are practising that
phrase. Muckers (or mucks) = mates, as
yes = hello, remember?)

Of course if it's private stuff we can
use email and we can text, within
reason. I mean, within credit limits.

Ah well, next summer I will be old enough
to get a part-time job. If there are any.

Enough recession depression!

Nite nite,
Aimée

'Night night,' echoed Clio as I climbed into bed. 'And Aimée – *do* get that screen saver changed. The lad might be embarrassed.'

Mañana, mother dear. *Mañana*. It's already in hand.

*

Text from Beks.

The O'Hara family are delighted to
announce the safe arrival at 10:55pm
of Jacob, a much-loved brother for
Rebekah, Hannah, Rachael, Ruth, Sarah
and Elizabeth. 6 pounds, 12 ounces.

Jacob O'Hara. Jake? I hope he likes yellow. More nappies, more walking the floor. More smiles, more cuddles.

I wonder if Beks is happy? Like, really happy?

Chapter
Ten

onday 24th. Seven days to go, still counting.

The sixth form study had been re-arranged to comprise a veritable Venn diagram of interlocking and overlapping seating spaces. I say 'rearranged', which suggests that I knew what it looked like before it was designated – much to the sixth form's disgust – as the Knockgorey Liaison Room.

But I didn't know what it was supposed to look like. Nor did any of us. I'd poked my head round the door a few times (on teachers' business) and it looks like anywhere you see a collective of sixth form. Overgrown lads with their feet up on the furniture and an earphone dangling, reading *GQ* and the footy pages, and intense-looking girls poring over Internet articles on Life Coaching, Food Combining and Finding Your Inner Self while painting their nails and drinking squash out of coffee mugs. (It was a delight indeed when we found they'd lost their battle to have a kettle and microwave. Health and safety again. After all, would you trust eighteen-year-olds with boiling water?)

But I digress.

Apart from the fact that the polished wood floor was clearly visible (i.e. minus the customary two-inch layer of crisp bags and chocolate wrappers, screwed-up pages of file paper, pencil shavings – eyebrow and 2B – and the detritus of a floating population fine-tuning their student slovenliness), it was probably much the same.

Apart from Mizz H, who was garbed in multicoloured floral tights, a denim skirt of almost indecent brevity and a smile. She stood, poised for action, in front of a display board onto which she had clipped a thick pile of sheets of off-white cheapo recycled paper. She was brandishing a red indelible marker which, I deduced, was the same pen which had been used to scrawl the banner headline 'Together for a Shared Future', which is typical of the phrases that feature in our school website and annual report when they can't think of anything new to say but want to sound aspirational and inclusive.

'Who he?' Bree whispered and nudged me in the ribs. I followed her eyes to a slight figure standing to Mizz's right. Male, arty looking, maybe early thirties. Dark, bearded. Lightly tanned. Good jeans. No socks. Faintly (and I stress faintly) Jack Sparrow. Without the earring. Clio would have described him as 'lightly made up'. Gran would have said he needed a decent feed.

Mizz H, you may recall, is small of body if not of volume so, in a strange way, they looked in proportion. Like a matching pair of sample-sized teachers.

'This is Mr Lynch from Knockgorey,' Mizz announced, startling the whispering one who thought she'd been overheard. 'He's come as a kind of ... advance party.'

'Nick Lynch,' he confirmed in an RTÉ continuity announcer's mellow tones. 'Head of Drama and Transition Year Co-ordinator. Call-me-Nick.'

The voice. OhmyGod. Another one. If the population of Ireland is approximately six million and half of them are male, and of that half, two-thirds have a brogue like that, then I have a serious weak spot in my moral armour.

'Mr Lynch,' Mizz continued, all sparkle and vibrancy, 'has just spent the weekend with me.'

Now, obviously that was inviting a chorus of giggles. To fail to provide same would only have disappointed and defined her as a forlorn and ageing spinster of the parish. A muted, measured attempt at laughter was forthcoming, underneath which Simon C-K could be heard expounding his familiar theory that Mizz was either spoken for or gay, as she had once refused the generous and unselfish offer he had made her at an outdoor pursuits event. No strings attached.

Simon C-K doesn't do rejection.

'And now, when you have formed yourselves into the appropriate clusters, Mr Lynch will move around and try to answer any questions you may have about the project.

So can I have twinned hosts to the middle, with twinned hosts who are also on the Columban float to the very front middle, Columban float but not hosting or twinned to the middle front right …'

The foreshortened arms were flapping like manic windmills and after much shuffling and pushing I found myself perched on the arm of a chair which was sort of middle-left-middle. Rebekah, I noted, was safely on the middle-front-right, where she belonged, and Bree was within heavy breathing distance of Mr Lynch (zone un-specified). Already I could hear her animated tones introducing herself as the Headline Act. Nary a word about the Headline Act's manager, I noted, but before I could mentally draft my resignation Mizz was squeezing herself between me and Patricia Wannabe Mooney to ask if we'd be up for saying a few words about our thoughts and experiences so far. She was sorry she hadn't had a chance to mention it to us earlier, she smiled apologeti-cally, but she knew we were more than capable.

I'm a sucker for a compliment. And there was no way la Mooney was taking centre stage. So, without further ado, I agreed to share my few words with the assembled company. After checking that it was acceptable to admit to having been in phone contact.

'Reverend sirs …' I began. It was unlikely that there were any but I included them out of courtesy, just in case. 'Reverend sirs, ladies and gentlemen, fellow members of the Twinning Committee, fellow pupils …'

Time for a bit of gravitas.

'I am honoured to stand before you today at this defin-ing moment in the history not only of Castle Grove but in the whole ethos of cross-border and cross-community co-operation. The Twinning Committee is proud and honoured to lead us, the Children of the Peace, in this innovative and ground-breaking exercise in building a shared future on this island. We thank those behind the scheme for their inspiration, their humanity and their vision.'

Mizz was beaming. This was going rather well.

'We are proud to extend a warm Derry welcome to those who share our beliefs and ideals in the hope of building lasting friendships. It is my aspiration that these will continue to enrich our lives in the years ahead when our days at Castle Grove are confined to memory. A cherished memory, as we aspire to live out all it stands for, in our daily life.'

Maybe I should include a few more pauses, for impact.

'Get on with it.'

Hark! Dissent in the ranks. I remained unfazed by hecklers.

'I hope you will forgive me, as I stand here before you today, if I suggest that it is not only the former British Prime Minister Tony Blair who has felt the Hand of History on his shoulder.'

I looked round my captive audience and savoured the power.

'Inclusivity. Embracing change. Challenging preconceptions. These are not mere buzz words, they are the moral framework for a new and better society in which every citizen will enjoy mutual respect and understanding, regardless of faith or tradition, ethnic origin, gender, sexual orientation, economic status ...'

(This was going rather well, I felt.)

'... where we, the Children of the Peace, the new Irelanders, may look to the wider world for our inspiration and address our contentious issues on a global scale ... Let us embrace change and embrace it with enthusiasm ...'

*

'Jeez, Aimée. What were you like? Some of us have things to do, our break to get, a life to lead. Come on.' Steven McQuillan is one of life's moaners. I didn't really expect more than one round of applause from my peers but, really, this was uncalled for.

'What's your problem?'

'Look – Mizz Hardy asked for a few words, not a bloody lecture. I've lost out on half a period with Mr MacDonnell already and I really want to get my planing finished today.'

'Some people,' I remarked in a loud aside to Rebekah, 'have no sense of occasion. Is it my fault if they cannot feel the Hand of History. How long was I?'

'Not that long.'

'How long?'

'I wasn't really timing it.'

'Beks.'

'Oh all right, then. About twenty-three minutes. But I only noticed cause Carly Jenkins was behind me and she was busting for a pee.

'But it was very good,' she added loyally. 'Very informative. And quite personal.'

Personal?

'You know – all that stuff about how the visit would mean different things to different students and how some had much more to gain or lose than others. That was about Darren, wasn't it?'

'No. Yes. I don't know.'

I was aware of a presence at my side.

'Excuse me.'

Mr call-me-Nick Lynch. With Mizz Hardy encroaching on his personal space.

'Yes?' I felt my features assuming the artless smile which, Bree says, makes me look Special. (That's Special, as in Educational Needs, not special, as in, well, special.)

'I just wanted to say how much I enjoyed your address. I can't believe it was impromptu, but Faustina tells me you have a natural aptitude for public speaking.'

I watched Simon C-K's jaw drop in disbelief. Faustina. There's a contraceptive of a name if ever I heard one. We always assumed the F was for Frances, or Fiona, or something more cosmopolitan and 21st century.

Mizz smiled through gritted teeth. 'Aimée has acquitted herself admirably in the Year 12 debates. Her mother is a parent governor,' she added brightly.

Why bring Clio into it?

'She has very generously agreed to host both Cassidy siblings, even though,' she added sweetly, 'Darren is in sixth year and isn't officially part of the exchange project. But in the circumstances …'

'Yes, indeed, very thoughtful. And inclusive.' Nick smiled with genuine warmth.

What circumstances?

'It hasn't been too difficult making the necessary adjustments to your home?' He was all polite concern.

'Oh no.' I smiled just as sweetly. 'My father has provided us with a camp bed which he bought for a previous incumbent and has never used.'

Nick looked puzzled.

'For Darren Cassidy,' I added. Did he need an interpreter? Foxrock isn't that far away and Caoimhe and Darren can understand me fine.

'Oh, I see. That's good.' He nodded sagely.

The walkabout and pressing of flesh continued with all the zeal of an opposition candidate at the hustings, leaving us to plan the next rehearsals. Plus, of course, our own personal agendas for the visit.

Rebekah was supervising the erection of the backdrop for the float that night.

'Why don't we stay on after Majorettes and help?' Bree asked.

Beks and I looked at each other in surprise. Bree? With a free evening? I made a quick mental inventory. No, she hadn't delegated her homework. Yet.

'Come on, Aimée, it's Clio's salsa night. We might as well. Then we could all go back to your place,'

'Not for long,' Rebekah interrupted. 'I promised I'd be home for the ten o'clock feed. But it'd be great,' she added happily. 'Tom says the float's really coming together. Though we do still need a few more volunteers for the tableau. As Tom says, reliable ones.'

She looked pointedly at Bree. But surely she is a gangsta sista? What is going on here?

'Perhaps you would suggest that to Caoimhe Cassidy?' Mizz H can be very light on her feet when she chooses to eavesdrop. 'You'd have spare skirts and cloaks, wouldn't

Felicity McCall

you, Rebekah? And it'd be one less thing for Mrs Logan – I mean, Ms McCourt, to worry about. It'd be very appropriate,' she added. 'You can go along with her, Aimée.'

Don't mind me, then. I'll just go with the flow. Actually, it sounded better than anything Clio and I had dreamed up so far. Even if it was only 'appropriate'.

'That's settled then.'

Her face must have been tired from all the smiling. Was this a foretaste of a more mature Mizz, post-Botox?

'And Aimée, I know your mother will get in touch if the arrangements pose any problems. Won't she?'

I nodded in assent. Then I had an idea. I asked her retreating back, 'Mizz Hardy? What about Darren Cassidy? Do you want him on the float too?'

What better way to travel the highways and byways incognito than disguised as a Celtic swineherd? And what better way for us to keep an eye on him? Derry women can be *so* predatory.

*

It looked very impressive, the float, even if I say so myself. Tom and Rebekah clearly made a good organising committee. Between them I reckoned they could stage a coup and take over the daily administration of Castle Grove, no problem. As a first stage in world domination, it wasn't bad. Even if it involved such mundane tasks as a joint mission to hunt the industrial-size stapler.

Beks (unlike my other BF) was not a mouth about her male friends but I sensed fellow feeling between them in terms of time management, multitasking and commitments *chez eux*. And intuition told me Tom's commitments might not have been as much fun as an O'Hara State Outing to McDs.

'That's just cause we both think Griffin's a pain,' Bree suggested. 'We pity anyone unfortunate enough to call him brother. Don't read so much into things, Aimée. You can be such a drama queen, you know.'

A more ridiculous case of the pot calling the kettle black would be hard to imagine. I ignored her, though. I'd been mulling over Mizz and call-me-Nick's constant remarks about the arrangements for the Cassidys. I felt like I was missing something. Never trouble trouble till trouble troubles you, Gran would advise.

She's probably right.

Probably.

Possibly.

'So where's Paul tonight?'

No point in beating about the bush. Cut to the chase and all that.

'Round at Brendy's. He's just up the road from him. He invited me, too, but to be honest I couldn't be arsed.'

This sounded like an invitation to talk. I am my mother's daughter, after all.

'What are they doing?'

'Nothing. As usual. They never do anything. I told Paul I'm getting fed up with rejection,' Bree added obliquely.

'But he hasn't rejected you. He asked you round.'

'Not that sort of rejection. Every weekend's the same, Aimée,' she confided. 'We talk about where we're going and they get all hyped up and say Jaguar, or Makarena, and when Carly and I ask what are we doing about ID, there'll be some friend of Paul's who's bought one in a pub for twenty quid or Infectious Mickey says he's borrowing his cousin's and his girlfriend's and we get all dressed up and they get a carry-out and then we spend an hour in the freezing cold waiting for some bloke dressed up in a monkey suit with an IQ in double figures and an NVQ Level One in Door Consultancy to laugh in our faces. And by then the taxi queues are streets long and it's another hour in the freezing cold and probably the rain before we get home. And all the time they're mouthing off and acting like hard men and talking about what they're going to do when they meet him in daylight and all that crap. And next week they'll do it all over again. It's pathetic.'

'And?'

'What do you mean, *and*?'

'There has to be an and.'

'Don't say anything ...'

I nodded. If Bree confides in me she will also confide in someone else and the source of any leak will not be traceable.

'Last week Brendy had a fair bit of drink in him and he threatened the gorilla on the door at Jaguar. It was *so* embarrassing. Like, the bloke would have killed him, for a start, and you don't threaten the blokes on the door at Jaguar. They look out for each other. And,' she added nonchalantly, 'Sorcha says they're all coke heads. I wouldn't be surprised.'

Nor would I, but I sensed it was the humiliation that was getting to my emergent sophisticate.

'Then Cretinous Barry got stuck in. For God's sake. Why they let him tag along I do not know. They look like silly wee boys and they can't see it,' Bree went on. 'And then they expect us to back them up and flatter their wee bruised egos. Frankly I've more to do with my time.

'At least at the Firewall,' she added, 'you get to dance.' She paused. 'At primary school they used to call Paul "Bungalow",' Bree confided, emboldened by the evening's bonding. 'It drives him pure mental. Brendy had to explain it to him,' she added gleefully. 'You know, looks good but nothing upstairs.'

*

Beks is putting the finishing touches to the backdrop.

'Here, hold that taut, Aimée. And staple. The job's a good one.'

It was. We stood back and surveyed the panoramic view of the Foyle, interspersed with panels depicting scenes from Colmcille's life. A music score had been tran-scribed in the background and the whole backdrop was decorated with Celtic symbols and St Brigid's crosses.

'I'm not sure that Columba and Brigid were contem-poraneous,' Rebekah whispered, 'but it does look really well.'

'Let's finish it tomorrow.' Bree was all enthusiasm. 'All we need is some artificial grass for the banks of the Foyle and we can mark out where everyone is supposed to sit with gaffer tape.'

'Tom can't do Wednesdays.'

'Just tomorrow,' Bree wheedled.

'He has a commitment on Wednesdays.'

Rebekah's tone was decisive. I got the feeling she knew more than she was letting on and she was keeping it to herself. Be like that, then, Rebekah.

But Bree couldn't let it rest. 'What's so important he can't leave it for once? We're volunteering our services here.'

'Leave it, Bree.'

'Come on, Beks.'

Rebekah was chilly. 'Just because you hadn't a better offer for tonight?'

That was a bit too close to home for Bree. 'Well, why not, then? Tell us. Aimée, don't kick me.'

Tact is not among Bree's finer qualities.

Silence. I looked round. Most of the volunteers were drifting away, out of earshot. Then Tom stepped down from his ladder and came over to us. He spoke clearly, quietly.

'I can't do Wednesdays because I go to Al Anon. My mum has a problem. Dad goes with me. They separated years ago, like, but he still goes. It's for families. It helps. End of story. Now leave it.'

Bree had the grace to look mortified. 'I didn't mean to be nosy. I mean, Sorcha and Willie are separated too, and so are Aimée's, and –'

'Leave it,' Tom said quietly. 'We all have a life outside Castle Grove, Bree. I just don't talk much about mine. For the record, my brother doesn't keep that well, either. As people are usually all too ready to point out. But I only talk about it to a few people. Special people.'

And he looked at Rebekah and smiled shyly. Without another word, Tom stepped down and walked away from the float and Rebekah followed.

Somehow, after that, it seemed unlikely that we would be gathering at my house to discuss Hallowe'en plans. Not then. Possibly not ever again?

'How was I to know?' Bree muttered, still clearly embarrassed. 'I mean, I'll tell anybody anything about my life and about our house. They only have to ask.'

I took her arm in a gesture of solidarity. Bree's heart is in the right place; it's just her brain that's a bit of a free radical.

'Come back with me,' I pressed her. 'Leave Beks and Tom alone for a while.'

'Is there curry?' She brightened instantly. 'Or brownies? What time does Clio get back?'

'Around ten, no curry, possibly some brownies left,' I promised. 'Rainbow doesn't rate them, so they're relatively safe. And we can go online and try to get Caoimhe on Facebook.'

'Or Darren,' she added, even more brightly, her recent blunder totally forgotten. Is this nature or nurture? I don't know. 'That's a thought.' Bree's evening was clearly looking up. 'I want another perv at the lovely Darren. Especially if I'm going on Facebook to him. You haven't deleted the screen saver, have you? You really ought to borrow Clio's webcam,' she added as an afterthought. 'They're very useful.'

Oh no oh no oh no. A suddenly single Bree looking for a deep and meaningful man was the last thing I needed this Hallowe'en.

Chapter
Eleven

F acebook time. Let's see who's on. Glad that Caoimhe and the girls are Facebook friends now so we can chat together, all cosy, like.

Caoimheimneverwrong: What did u think of our Mr Lynch?

earthmotherBeks: Caoimhe did u know he was coming he seems gr8. Can't wait to meet u.

Caoimheimneverwrong: I knew cos he cancelled Friday night's drama. He's

```
really good, giving up part of his
weekend for those of us that need a bit
of extra help!
```

I joined in. Inclusion, remember? The byword of Castle Grove.

```
Aimée: Hi Beks hi cc good to hear from u
y doesn't he wear sox?

Caoimheimneverwrong: Something to do
with reflexology, I think. BTW, I'm
happy to go on the float. Have white
blouse and pumps if u do skirt? Am small
— size 6 to 8.

earthmotherBeks: I'm 8 so no probs.

Aimée: I h8 stick insects!!

Caoimheimneverwrong: Darren's not sure
about costume. Wot do u think?

earthmotherBeks: Tell him all t lads do.

Aimée: Tell him to come online.

Caoimheimneverwrong: says nah it's full
of skangers.

earthmotherBeks:Wot?

Aimée: Yeh wot?

Caoimheimneverwrong: Skangers.
```

Juveniles.

Aimée: Ah wee wains.

earthmotherBeks: Yep. Tell him he can b
a chieftain or a swineherd.

Caoimheimneverwrong: ??

earthmotherBeks: On t float.

Caoimheimneverwrong: Maybe. sez he wl
talk to u tomorrow Aimée. Nite xx

So, I asked myself:

1
Why is she saying 'night night' at half past
nine? Does she have more important things to do?
I trust not ...

2
Why does she get extra help with drama? She
sounds very bright. But it explains call-me-
Nick and Friday nights. All legitimate.

3
Are the practice of reflexology and wearing
socks mutually exclusive?

4

Why am I surrounded by stick insects?
Are they naturally programmed to seek out
larger mammals for companionship?

5

Why is Darren going to talk to me about his
costume? Does this mean we have bonded?

Memo to self (a):

Bree really should give GoPual one last
chance. Must counsel her when we are visiting
Jacob O'Hara in the afternoon and ensure she
is offside for the Darren phone call.
(She even sounds glamorous.
How unfair is that?)

Memo to self (b):

Warn Clio of impending Bree charm offensive
re: borrowing webcam. Allude to worrying long-
term health implications etc. as in campaign
against mobile phone masts.

<u>Memo to self (c):</u>

Approach Rebekah with caution after the Tom debacle.

<u>Memo to self (d):</u>

Ask Clio about Al Anon.
Or, better still, read the website.

*

Mrs O'Hara sat like a Renaissance Madonna in the middle of her brood, deftly hemming dirndl skirts (they were going as the von Trapps – you know, *The Sound of Music* and all that?) while the latest addition slept contentedly in his crib.

We added our little yellow (me) and white (Bree) towelling thingies to the pile of little yellow and white towelling thingies.

Jacob remained peaceful, if all decked out in unsuitable pink. Well, they've got to recycle, haven't they? Even if it causes gross misunderstandings when Rebekah has him out in the buggy. People can be so sexist. I had lots of blue – Clio preferred it.

'So, had the hospital changed much from the last time you were in, Mrs O'Hara?'

What sort of inane conversational gambit was this from Bree? Not to mention tactless.

'Not really, love, but then I hardly got a look at it. He almost arrived at – what was it, Rebekah? – about half past nine at night when we were out in the twenty-four hour Tesco's doing a big weekly shop before school. And before I forget,' she addressed this to me, 'I said, I must say to Aimée about her father's lady friend. She's really nice. I think that's three times I've met her now. Over at the clinic. Fiona, isn't it? I recognised your dad when he dropped her off, one time. And then we got talking.'

It's amazing how one's focus can shift. The possible procreation had rather slipped my mind. But if possibly pregnant Fiona was in the same batch as Mrs O'H, then surely that made her imminent?

Memo to self: ring Dad. Asap. No point in being coy. Look where the direct approach got me with Darren.

Oblivious to the panic her casual remark had caused, Mrs O'H turned her attention to Bree. 'I must give your mum a ring. I'm looking to borrow a pair of lederhosen for Mr O'Hara. Nothing too fancy. I know she knows a lot of theatricals. It's just for the one night. He's doing extra shifts at the minute but I'll make sure he tries them on before-hand to check the fit. He's a thirty-six short, not that that matters with lederhosen. Oh, and braces. I'd like the em-broidered ones if she has them. With the wee flowers on.'

Edelweiss?

Jacob woke at this point and was duly passed round and cooed and clucked over and Bree and I made a polite exit.

'Do you think they'll stop now they've got a boy?' she asked as we walked down the street.

'Don't be so sexist,' I retorted, having just been won-dering the exact same thing. 'That would imply that Hannah right through to Elizabeth were mistakes.'

We continued in silence.

'Do you think we upset Beks about Tom? I mean, I haven't said anything to anybody –'

'There's nothing to say,' I interjected.

'Yes, exactly. I mean, it's shit that his mum's a bit of an alky but he's probably talking it up a bit. To get sympathy. Typical bloke. Look, all parents – OK, *most* – most of our parents like a drink. It's a fact of life. They can't hold it any more and they get legless. You've seen Sorcha and her mates after a girlie night out. It's not good. And look at the men they pick up when they have the beer goggles on. Gross.'

'Bree. It is not the same thing.'

'She gets out of her tree, Aimée. You know she does. One time she –'

'Bree. It is not the same thing. OK?'

'Sorr-ee.' Bree was miffed.

'Well, it isn't. So just leave it.'

'And you would know?'

'I looked up Al Anon. And I did collect all the leaflets the time we did safe drinking limits in health and social care,' I added in what I knew was a very condescending tone.

'So did I, if you remember, and I can tell you I've seen Sorcha drink her week's safe units in one night. Like at Audrey Lester's hen party. Sorcha said those leaflets were a pile of shite,' she added helpfully.

'Bree! It is not the same! Trust me. Or ask Clio,' I added. 'It's bound to feature in women's studies somewhere. Causes and effects, that sort of stuff. Lifestyle issues. Impact on the family.'

Except that's the theory. The academic stuff.

For Tom it was for real.

We walked on in silence. At the corner, Bree turned for home.

'I think I'll go back and have a shower. I want to be ready in good time. I think I should give Paul one last chance.'

'Great idea!' I responded, too quickly. 'See how it goes. That's more than fair,' I enthused before heading rapidly in the opposite direction. I was (tentatively) expecting a phone call.

And sure enough, at one minute past ten, the phone rang. Clearly a creature of habit. Dependable, even?

'Hey.'

'Hiya.'

We exchanged brief pleasantries.

'You really must get Caoimhe to set you up on Facebook,' I reminded Darren. 'It'd save you a fortune in phone calls. I presume you do use a mobile?'

'I told you, Aimée, I'm not into the Internet the way my sister is. It suits her, y'know?'

No mention of the skangers, I noted. Good, good. And how did he do that with his voice? My name had never sounded more attractive.

'So …' I broached the alleged subject of the call. 'How are you fixed for a costume? Do you want Beks and me to go ahead and get you sorted? And if so, would you rather be a chieftain or a swineherd? I'd go for swineherd. If I was you, I mean.' Gabble, gabble.

Pause.

'There's no point in trying to bullshit you, Aimée, is there?'

'Not a lot, no,' I concurred. 'Even though you tried before.' The Cassidys would be here in less than a week. There was no point in being disingenuous.

'I don't really want to go on the float.'

'Why? You've no one to go up the town with. You'll be left standing round like a spare part.'

Silence. Long silence. I could feel my bullshit detector activating.

'What would you do instead, Darren? When we're on the float? I mean, I haven't signed up for it – officially, anyway – but since Caoimhe's going on it, I'll be going with her.'

Silence. Again. Like he hadn't got a plan B.

'I was just thinking, Aimée, it might not be right, y'know? I'm not really part of the exchange thing. I'm not sure if I should be up there in public with the rest of you and –'

'Darren. No.'

'No?'

'No. The real reason. Please. Have the decency to tell me.'

Another long pause. Was he bracing himself to tell me or was he making something up?

Then that laugh. That smile in the voice. Mellow. There's a word.

'OK. No bullshit, Aimée, OK?' Another chuckle. 'Promise you won't be offended?' Try me. But he was at his most persuasive as he went on. 'It's because, like, it all sounds very worthy. But boring. Totally boring. I know you have to do that sort of thing to keep the funders happy and to get the publicity but if I don't have to, why should I? It's hardly a good night's craic.'

'Thanks.' Some of us might enjoy it.

'Well, tell me, would you be stuck on the float with a crowd of juveniles if your friends were free to hang around town with you? I don't think so.'

Touché, Darren.

'That's not the point. It's about the spirit of co-operation.' I tried to sound superior. And failed. Miserably.

'And it'll be the only chance I'll get to have a look round on my own, Aimée. To do a bit of exploring, y'know? I want to get talking to people. Get a sense of the place. The Derry vibe. Whatever.'

Whatever.

'I mean,' he wheedled, 'apart from Hallowe'en night itself, the whole timetable is organised for us by the schools. They'll decide where we go and who we meet. It'll be non-negotiable. I just fancy a bit of space, Aimée. D'you understand?'

Too right I did.

'Darren, there's nothing to stop you getting the bus up to Derry any Saturday,' I reasoned, 'if you want to see the city. I'd be happy to show you round.' Understatement. 'But I know what the town's like at Hallowe'en,' I tried to reason. 'Loads of people up there will be off their faces, and it'll get worse once the family-friendly stuff is over and the serious partying starts. And even if you make friends, you won't recognise them again. You won't know what they look like. They'll all be dressed up. Their own mothers wouldn't recognise them.'

Cringe. Engage brain, Aimée, before opening mouth. Please.

No, actually, Aimée, it's OK. Carry on. He is being stupid, rude and a bit of a fantasist. Aka male.

'I mean, what exactly are you planning on doing?'

Yet another long pause. I could wait.

'Aimée.'

'Yeah?'

'If I go on the float …'

I don't do deals.

'It's your choice. You can go on the float or you can sit in our house on your own. Clio wouldn't be happy about you wandering the streets,' I improvised. 'And everyone will be up the town. Really. Even my gran goes up the town at Hallowe'en. I don't want you going around making a total prat of yourself,' I appealed. 'It's not fair on Clio.'

'All I was going to say was, if I go on the float, will you help me? And get your mam and your mates to help me?'

'With your costume?'

'Eh … yeah. My costume. I'm a bit embarrassed about the whole thing. I don't really *do* fancy dress. And I'm not into drama like Caoimhe is.'

Why did I detect relief in his voice? Did I want to know?

'The home economics department and the art department should be able to sort you out. There must be spares. Or they can run something up. I'll check it out for you. And if the worst comes to the worst, Clio's great at things like that. It'll be dead easy. The costumes are very basic, you know.'

'That is really good of you. I appreciate it. Thanks for understanding, Aimée. I feel a bit stupid now. I feel I can trust you not to make a show of me.'

And I felt I couldn't trust you as far as I'd throw you, Darren Cassidy. But if my resolve was wavering now, I knew I hadn't a hope once he was up here.

'I'm sure we'll get space to work on it,' I said, trying not to sound (a) pervy/keen to see him in his underbags or (b) sad.

'That'd be good. That'd be really good, Aimée.'

Ay-mee. It sounds so lyrical when he says it. Softer. Devoid of the harsh northern nasal. Thank you, Clio, for not calling me Faustina.

Chapter Twelve

I woke on Monday 31st in a very peculiar mood. Could this be a panic attack? Jumpy stomach, clumsy fingers, unruly hair (nothing new there, then). This whole exchange (Darren) thing had my sleep patterns wrecked. I was not getting my requisite REM period.

Memo to self for November

1

'Realign bed to ensure am sleeping with magnetic north going through my big toe.
This is supposed to help.

2

Actually find magnetic north.

3

And find out its importance in restful and energising sleep.
Consult Clio/Sorcha/Gran/Google.

4

Ask Clio about homoeopathic sleep remedies and how much they cost.

The Mammy seemed equally disengaged from reality that morning, until I realised she was saving her lenses for an all-nighter and was blissfully unaware of the trail of cat hairs, crunchy salmon 'n' tuna pieces, slopped coffee and gel pen marks she was leaving in her wake as she chased Rainbow round the kitchen with his grooming brush while trying to multitask by ingesting her third caffeine fix of the day and writing random notes about notes on her yellow Post-it pad in preparation for the arrival of the Knockgorey Two.

The radio was tuned not to Radio 4, her frequency of choice, but to the local station where Mizz Hardy was to be interviewed about cross-border co-operation.

I thought they might have liked to speak to a host twin on the show, too, just to balance things, but then I suppose I wouldn't have had time for Rebekah to come round and fix my hair and (discreet) make-up.

And where *was* Rebekah? This was no time for Jacob O'Hara to discover colic nor for Mr O'Hara to have a personal crisis while considering the wisdom of parading the city streets of his hometown in creaky lederhosen with a 'Souvenir of Switzerland' Alpenhorn slung round his neck.

'Will I put on your toast? Aimée! She's on now!'

Clio turned up the volume to drown out the pitiful miaowing of the neglected one and together we listened to Mizz trying to cram the maximum number of buzz-words and funders' catchphrases into every ninety-second reply. Her 'twinning counterpart' Mr Lynch was supposed to be on the line from Monaghan (OhmyGod, halfway there already) but the line kept dropping out.

Granny grew up there and she reckons that particular part of our borderland has its own microclimate and signal system as well as a unique subculture and gene pool. It's all down to the bad winters in the hills, she says. Whole communities used to being snowed in from Christmas to Easter, if she's to be believed, with only the milk lorry making intermittent contact with the outside world. It is not conducive to positive mental health and well-being or the functioning of satellite dishes and Xboxes.

Ringringring at the door and I rushed to answer it, expecting Rebekah.

'Dad.'

At 08.20? Washed, shaved and with his car parked outside and a photographer waiting in the passenger seat?

'Is your mam here?'

'Well, naturally ...'

'Clio. A quick word. I'm meeting the bus when it arrives at Castle Grove.'

'They're in Monaghan now, at the bog stop –'

'Wait a minute, Aimée. I need a word with your mam.'

No sense of occasion, my parents.

I picked up Rainbow and retreated to my room to switch on my straighteners. Hurry up, Rebekah, I thought as I looked into my mirror.

Maybe just another thin layer of pan stik.

Rainbow. Give it back. Now. You are *so* not a Soft Ivory.

I heard the door close. Loudly. It was the Da leaving to continue with his honest day's pursuit of items of alleged interest. That would start a few rumours among the neighbours.

'Aimée!'

Yeah, I knew, get a move on.

I texted Beks:

Where r u? x urgent

'Aimée, quick! I need a word. Now!'

I recognised that tone. Something majorly serious had happened. And it was, inexplicably, deemed to be my fault.

'Aimée!'

Clio looked … not angry, not upset, more what Granny would call 'flummoxed'. Her voice was remarkably calm, her tone measured.

'Think back to the day you came home with the first twinning pack. The one with Caoimhe's personal profile and her school's exchange letter and all the Castle Grove handouts with times and dates and things.'

'Yeah.'

'What did you do with them?'

'They're in the file box on your desk. We checked them last night. You remember.'

This was no time for the woman to lose her grip on reality. Or experience the early onset of post-menopausal senility.

'We went through them together,' I explained in my most patronising voice.

'Not last night. When you first brought them home.'

'I read them and then you read them. You remember, the girls were here. Rebekah was, anyway, to start with, which is more than she is now.'

'Aimée. This is important.'

More important than my frizz? That was important.

'Think carefully. Was that them all?'

'Yes.'

'Do you remember a green-coloured supplement?'

'No. Wait ...'

There had been so much of the stuff. And it was so repetitive. They couldn't seriously have expected us to read it all. Could they?

'I don't think so.'

'About four A4 pages. Green.'

'Why?'

A mental picture was developing. It was of Bree, her legs stuck out at right angles, waiting for her fake tan to develop. And, spread neatly over the stools and floor, under her outstretched thighs, were sheets of paper. Lifted, no doubt, from our recycling pile in the corner. Green paper.

'Bree's legs!' I squealed. 'She had paper spread out under her legs. When she was fake tanning them. I think it was green.'

'Are you sure?'

'No. But I do remember green pages. She must have taken them from the recycling pile.'

'And someone must have put them there to be recycled.'

'Ah.'

'Aimée, if I was one hundred per cent sure we never got that supplement I would ring your Mizz Hardy and give her a large piece of my mind. But I can't be, can I?'

'Well ... no.'

Clio was definitely flummoxed. Distraught. As far out of her comfort zone as the night we thought Rainbow had lapped up an entire and generous glass of Chablis, but it turned out to be Jilly drinking a man right out of her hair at double speed.

'Because,' she continued, her voice gathering momentum, 'your dad called past to tip me off about this, which was very good of him. He's been asked to concentrate on a couple of individual students in his twinning feature. Ones where the student has a special reason for coming and the host family has, as his editor put it – not very originally either – "gone the extra mile".'

'Not Darren the Troubled Teen?'

How could that story have got out? Bree? Worse still, me? Don't be ridiculous. All teens are troubled.

'No,' she paused for effect, 'they want a profile on Caoimhe Cassidy, a vibrant young girl who lives life to the fullest … and uses a wheelchair. Juvenile rheumatoid arthritis.' Clio looked me straight in the eye.

It was a good thing we lived on the ground floor. And that I didn't give voice to that thought. And that I had clearly inherited the coping strategies passed through the female McCourt line.

Now some of the more cryptic of the exchange leaders' remarks were becoming clear.

Oh.

But why had Caoimhe never mentioned it?

Then again, why would she? And while it shouldn't make any difference … would it?

*

Normal life at Castle Grove, if you'll forgive the contradiction in terms, had been suspended for forty-eight hours. It would have been seventy-two, but All Saints'

Day is a day of obligation, or recovery, depending on your observances at Hallowe'en, so it was a formal day off.

Arriving at school, I was greeted by a banner strung across reception, 'Castle Grove welcomes our Knockgorey Visitors', which was as unimaginative as it was inoffensive. Checking the spelling (mother's daughter again), I saw it had been mercifully spared the poster-paint ministrations of Carly Jenkins.

Clio could probably argue the case for and against Castle Grove being singular or plural, but the other source of my gene pool, who is less anally retentive about linguistics, was mercifully engrossed in interviewing anything and everything that had been drawn to his colleague's camera lens.

Well, he is quite cute. (Young Lensman Colleague, not the Da. Don't even go there.)

That was La Mooney taken care of, anyway. Flirt, pose, flirt. And then some.

The sixth-form study had been flung open to the elements with trestle tables from the canteen serving as a makeshift juice bar and administration centre and to wedge open the French windows. (Health and safety, anyone?) Mizz H was poring over an accumulation of files, clipboards, printed pages (none of them green, I noted) and fact packs to rival the Oval Office. Indeed, given her diminutive stature, it was really only her head and shoulders which were clearly visible as she bobbed up and down over the checklists.

I scanned the assembled masses for any sign of Beks. None. Bree was there, mercifully still pompom-free, talking to Rachael and –

And –

And if Rachael was in school, uniformed and ready, where was Rebekah?

I wasn't doubting Rachael's ability to wash and dress herself. She's eleven, for heaven's sake. But they always came on the bus together. *Always.*

Unless something was wrong.

Mizz H lifted the microphone and the shriek of distortion effectively drew our attention to her, the centrifugal force of this Defining Moment in our School's History. The principal was on a course (I think that's what they do); one vice-principal was off on the long-term sick having her bunions done and the other was representing us at an international conference on something or other. (Inclusive sport, I think.) This was Faustina Hardy's big moment and she intended to savour it.

Then someone unplugged her to get the tea urn boiling.

The full fury of her thwarted ambition was unleashed on two latecomers slinking in the back. Forty-eight pairs of eyes turned to look on the unfortunates.

Rebekah and Tom.

Rebekah is never late. She has one hundred per cent attendance certificates going back to P1. Thus, as I observed before, do rumours start.

I mouthed, 'What's up?' while I saw Bree blatantly scanning Beks' person for signs of damage which might render cheerleading impossible.

I saw Beks surreptitiously texting. This, too, was out of character.

I excused myself to go to the loo and read,

> Tom's mum n hospl. Hv to go back
> there. More l8r. Cn u run float? Tb

Could I run, float?

Could I … ah, I see. Could I organise the Columban float? Well, I could, but why?

I texted back,

Yes y?

and had just pressed send when I heard Bree's frenzied hammering on the loo door and the news that the bus was here.

*

It'd be easy to sneer and say 'get a life', but really it was quite exciting. Much more frenetic than a normal half-day. People were jumping up and down, waving their twins' photos and welcome packs and shouting up at the bus windows. The Cute Lensman snapped; the catering staff appeared with trays laden with scones and shortbread. Some idiot cut loose a bunch of balloons which floated away in the general direction of the soccer pitch. Two more seriously affected idiots burst into the opening lines of 'Danny Boy'. Suddenly people were stepping off the bus and everyone was cheering and hugging and air-kissing.

And call-me-Nick was introducing me to a delicate-looking fair-haired girl with an amazing smile, *sans* wheelchair, and a seventeen-year-old (nearly eighteen) whose physical presence was the stuff of which legends are made. And they were both hugging me. Very publicly.

Me, Aimée Logan. Aka the narrator.

Nice one, Mizz.

'You do look really like your picture,' I heard my voice remark (inanely.)

Well, I couldn't say, 'Where's your wheelchair?', could I?

But I did wonder if the Da and his editorial team had got it wrong. It's not unheard of.

Not so.

Within minutes, Darren was telling me in the most matter-of-fact way that the (folding) chair was in the coach's boot along with their bags and Caoimhe was saying she was going to use it as little as possible during the visit but her parents and the school had insisted she bring it anyway, which was only sensible.

'It is the proverbial elephant in the room,' she assured me with that disarming grin. 'That's why I was so glad I was twinned with you, Aimée. People mean well. But, you know, they ask terribly polite questions or go out of their way not to say something inappropriate. But you were amazing. Right from that first email. You just acted as if you didn't know about my JRA – my arthritis. You know, as if it made no difference.'

Well, I didn't, I thought, and it doesn't. Adults will insist on embarrassing us by being so overly PC that it's politically incorrect, if you get what I mean.

I was suddenly conscious of Caoimhe's Mr Lynch on my left and Bree on my right. Mr Lynch was quietly thanking me for being so thoughtful about the float and the costume, explaining how, for Caoimhe, making her way on foot through overcrowded streets wasn't an option. He also asked me to thank my dad for making his car available.

Bree was silently staring at Darren, all vestiges of subtlety cast aside. I mean, *staring*.

It would have been rude not to take a second look myself.

Bree's reaction was entirely in order. Indeed, in-evitable. His smile was as broad, his eyes as intensely magnetic, his skin as spot-free as the pic had suggested.

Forget airbrushing and digital enhancing; he was just one of those rare and envied individuals who looks ef-fortlessly, naturally, unnaturally good.

I tried to remind myself that there's a fine line between angst-ridden and brooding, and foul-tempered, self-centred and grumpy.

Caoimhe clearly doted on him.

Bree's response was much less emotional. Or whole-some.

Without any self-consciousness, Caoimhe gave us a brief and well-rehearsed summary of JRA. It was clearly a tedious ritual reassurance of the concerns of over-solic-itous adults. No, no one knew how or why she'd got it and no, no, it wasn't infectious or contagious, not that they, the PC adults, would even have suggested this, heavens above, no. And yes, exercise was good for her and yes, she might grow out of it. Or she might not. And that, Caoimhe told us with unexpected steely resolve, was that. Subject closed.

'I knew it wouldn't be an issue with you, Aimée.' The Vision beamed at me and squeezed my shoulder in a friendly (sadly, only friendly) way.

But – happy days. Bree made the mistake of attempt-ing a pseudo-intellectual question, insisting on a reply and then glazing over as soon as Darren's reply became in any way complex.

'He's too … what's that word Clio uses? Cerebral for me,' she would later say, to my intense relief, purring with pleasure at having remembered a three-syllable adjective.

The next couple of hours passed in a blur of a joint Powerpoint presentation by our leaders, juice and scones (organic), more juice and scones (last minute buy-ins from the corner shop, as demand was outstripping supply, and blatantly mass produced, even 'own brand').

Details of the evening's schedule were distributed, with copies for host parents. I even agreed to let the Cute Lensman take my pic between the Cassidys. (Temporary amnesia about frizz.) Then, Mizz reminded us, after school officially ended at one o'clock, Knockgorey delegates would have an opportunity to bond with their host family. I was about to ask Caoimhe and Darren what they'd like to do, when I heard my name mentioned from the microphone: 'Final rehearsal for the Columban float and costume fitting, facilitated by Aimée Logan. Participants, first aiders and Mr MacDonnell's woodwork squad to assemble at the tennis courts at twelve noon.'

'You didn't tell us you were in charge! That's brilliant,' Caoimhe exclaimed.

'I'm really just the standby facilitator for my friend Rebekah's friend Tom,' I added with false modesty.

'I'd better go to that, too,' Darren added, 'though that doesn't mean I'm committing to the float.'

'Yes, you are,' I assured him. 'Besides, we may be two down.'

I searched the crowds in vain for Tom 'n' Beks.

But Mizz must know they weren't there. And why.

At least Bree had the wit not to canvass us to replace her missing majorette. I saw her heading off, dejected, in the general direction of Carly Jenkins. Bree does not do humble pie.

I checked my phone.

> Thanx so much c u l8r ps need to contact Clio asap. Beks.

Something was wrong. Very wrong. And I knew what it was most likely to be.

Poor Tom's mum.

Poor Tom.

And I had no idea what to do. Except to consult Clio asap. Not to break confidentiality; just for advice.

And get that float ... floating?

Chapter Thirteen

sap would turn out to be half past one at the earliest.

I texted my mother:

> Rebekah needs 2 talk asap
> probs re Tom's mum c u 130x

But I didn't get a reply. That didn't surprise me as Clio usually keeps her phone off or on silent when she is in her office at the uni. She always says she gets her 'serious work' done when it's a student-free zone. (We get a day and a half for Hallowe'en. They get a week. How unfair is that?)

The rehearsal went really well, if I say so myself. Mind you, it was more a matter of running through the timetable and making sure everyone had been assigned a costume and knew which particular X of gaffer tape marked their spot. Totally unselfconsciously, Caoimhe told everyone she'd prefer to take her chair rather than risk having to drop out. The technology department knocked together a sort of improvised Celtic shrub and we draped and pinned the last of the green lining material over it so it would camouflage the chair a bit and blend seamlessly into Caoimhe's skirt and cloak.

She was right; she's so slim the skirt was huge on her but once we'd pinned it into place and wrapped her in her cloak, the effect was pretty good. I think I was a tad robust for mine but to have gone for the alternative Cleopatra look at the last minute would have been way too surreal. The nipped in waist was flattering, falling casually into soft folds over the hips to emphasise the curves, as the fashion pundits might enthuse. Hell, it was £2.99 a metre lining fabric. For one night. Who cares?

Besides, Clio informed me crisply when I arrived home, she and Jilly had reclaimed the wig and commandeered the brocade and were most definitely dressing up to mark the occasion, should they never set foot outside the house that night. (Unlikely in the extreme.) Tom's cloak was a bit short and skimpy for Darren but Bree assured Mizz that Sorcha would come to the rescue. Anyway, she and I had every confidence the previous incumbent (Tom) would be back to reclaim his part.

'Mizz seemed to agree. She just uh-huh-ed that,' I told Clio, as I gave Rainbow an extra-thorough flea check before the Knockgorey coach dropped off our guests at 1A Riverview. 'A sort of ambivalent grunt. Have you heard from Rebekah?'

Silence.

Oh.

'Confidentiality issues?'

'Something like that, yes.'

'Sorry. It's just you did say you knew Tom's mum or knew something about her ...'

'Aimée.' The tone was firm. 'Not even your father, in the extremes of his profession, would ask any more.'

'Sorry.'

'Rebekah did phone just before you came home,' she added. 'She thanked you for looking after the float and apologised for not getting a chance to meet Caoimhe and Darren today. She's a very mature young woman,' Clio added. 'Tom's lucky to have her to talk to.'

I only had time to blurt, 'And don't worry about the wheelchair,' and see Clio indicate a virtual textbook of print-outs on disability access, when the Knockgorey driver pulled up outside.

Closely followed by a taxi, from which emerged an imposing if elderly figure swathed in orange and red drapes, carrying a ghetto blaster and a cake tin. Closely followed by Eamonn's car, containing Eamonn and the Cute Lensman. Closely followed on foot by Bree and Sorcha.

I put the kettle on. An appropriate if inadequate response.

If my small but extended family deliberately set out to shame me by flaunting their eccentricities in public, I doubt they could have done a better job of it. What followed was an exercise in dysfunction. To précis this cringeworthy hour of insanity, it will suffice to say that Gran aka Fire Leader gave us a demonstration of her t'ai chi routine on the tarmac outside the apartment block. Unbidden. (In case we missed her in the square. How? Massed throngs of geriatric groupies besieging the Guildhall steps?)

Needless to say, this coincided with the daily arrival home of the commuting populace which comprised our neighbours. I reckon she'd taken out her hearing aid, too – that CD was *loud*, as well as odd. Vanity is a terrible thing. As is the need to … well, show off. I'm glad that's not hereditary either.

Of course Mister Cute Lensman had to have a pic as one of the two twinning stories had fallen through, the Da explained (Could it be La Mooney's? Tell me more … mental note – get Bree to one side for the gossip) and Lensman thought this was a winning image.

Fire Leader needed no second bidding. She was soon strutting her stuff while Mam served the (excellent if inebriated) fruit cake which was her contribution to the welcome, I handed round drinks and Sorcha and Bree cut and snipped and pinned and tucked a bolt of rough woven hessian-effect fabric round a protesting Darren. OK, not really protesting. Mildly enjoying, even. And it was Sorcha who cut, snipped, etc. while Bree looked on and commented. Favourably. Cheesily favourably.

I lobbed in a few incisive comments about gangsta sista's costume, which was an exercise in tackiness, but got no reaction.

Once Darren's cloak had been secured with a repro-
duction Tara brooch at his shoulder and had, in turn,
been captured on digital image for what promised to be
a Family Special Pull-Out Colour Supplement, I left him
and the Da deep in conversation about the possibility of
Eamonn taking us all for a scenic drive round Donegal
before they went back home and went off to help
Caoimhe unpack. Showing her the bathroom, I found
the furry fiend delivering the *coup de grâce* to the
welcome – sitting in the bath, peeing down the plughole,
as is his wont. Hearing Caoimhe's peal of laughter, the
Mammy came in and made some inane remark about
Rainbow thinking he's human.

If so, mother dear, who is he copying?

But the Cassidys seemed to be loving it.

'It's so relaxed here,' Caoimhe explained. 'Darren says
the same thing. I thought northerners were supposed to
be gritty and hard, or depressed and miserable?'

I stood with her at the kitchen door and looked at the
motley crew assembled round the table. Gritty?
Depressed? Worn down by years of post-trauma conflict
resolution?

'Maybe some of them?' I offered hopelessly.

The crowd dispersed, giving the hosts some quality
time with their guests. Bree dispersed with reluctance, I
might add. But I reminded – nay, threatened her about
the need to make a final check with GoPual and his band
of brothers about their arrangements. Or lack of them.

Clio ensured the Cassidys rang home to confirm their
safe arrival at 1A Riverview and from the very sincere but
undeniably formal exchanges, I could see that the

Cassidys must find the random McCourt-Logan interaction hard to understand.

Then Clio suggested that since we'd have a surfeit of
apple pie and barmbrack when we got back from the
Carnival, and that since no one had really had a proper
lunch, we should go for the easy option and get a take-
away asap. She then suggested ordering by phone and
that Darren and I go to collect it. Caoimhe immediately
agreed, all this, 'What a great idea, I am a bit tired,
y'know,' stuff until I felt it was a set up.

We agreed on the family special meal deal (D, with
extra prawn crackers and two litres of complimentary
Coke) and I heard Clio order more food than I had
known her to consume in the past month.

'Rebekah might call by,' she added (too) casually.
'She's so keen to meet you both and I expect she won't
have had time for any dinner.'

Definitely a set-up.

It's a good twenty minutes' walk each way, plus
waiting time, and no one mentioned the word taxi.

*

It actually took us more than half an hour to get to the
Mayflower Palace, partly because I kept stopping to point
out landmarks to Darren and partly because it was too
good an opportunity to miss being seen by as wide a cross-
section of the youth populace as possible.

He was, like I said, really easy to talk to. Without giving
away any confidences, he told me a bit about Caoimhe
being bullied at her national school and how things were
lots better now they were both at Knockgorey. He said
Caoimhe felt a lot of this was down to him fighting her

corner. Not that he could take the credit, he said; it was just that their parents were quite reserved and a bit in awe of the teaching profession. Deferential. They weren't ones to make a fuss or to raise issues with the school.

Knockgorey was great in lots of ways, he said; it'd really helped Caoimhe to come out of her shell and built up her confidence. In an eerie echo of Cliospeak, he was fulsome in his praise of call-me-Nick and the benefits of drama. I found myself saying all sorts of complimentary things about Castle Grove. Darren said it was class having a pet like Rainbow and thought my story about Clio and me measuring him and finding his hips were just an inch smaller than Victoria Beckham's was funny. He said he didn't like size zero women (bless him, bless him) and I promised not to pass on the story of how he actually dealt with one of Caoimhe's tormentors when she was in first year. So I won't. I respect people's confidences, you know. (Gratuitous violence – never. Strong and tough – yesss.)

He thought my gran was wonderful (most people do) and that it was class the way my parents got on with each other. (Do Foxrockers say 'class' a lot?) I agreed, adding quickly, 'but not while living under the same roof'.

On the way back, upping the pace lest our spring rolls and chow mein specials got cold, he broached his own particular elephant in the room – his ulterior motive or, as he put it, his personal reason for the visit.

'You know I haven't been getting on too well with my folks.'

'That's an understatement.'

He chuckled. 'Yeah, right. My mum and dad, they're good people, don't get me wrong ...'

That sounded strange, for a start.

'... nothing in common with them, y'know, but once I realised, I understood, like, it all made sense ...'

Pay attention, Aimée. Concentrate mind, not hormones.

'Explain what you mean, Darren, about it all making sense?'

(Tip from the Da: always ask an open question rather than one that can be answered yes or no.)

He held my shoulders firmly and spun me round to face him.

'I'm adopted.'

'Oh. Right. So?'

'I've only just discovered it.'

This didn't make sense. Everyone knows they're adopted these days. If they are, I mean. He was dreaming, had to be.

'Don't worry,' I gabbled, 'I thought that too when I was about nine and nothing – *nothing* – could convince me otherwise –'

'Cop on, Aimée, you're the image of your mum and dad. Mannerisms, everything.'

Thanks.

'Clio says it's quite common,' I rushed on. 'It's all about wanting to establish your own individualism, separate from the family dynamic –'

'You don't get it.'

His tone bore all the kind condescension of MacDonnell, my technology teacher, describing to me the mysterious practices of crafting a dovetail joint, a skill forever inaccessible to me, a fact which causes me no grief whatsoever.

'I *am* adopted, Aimée. I know. I've seen a copy of my birth certificate. It's not the original. It's an amended one. A copy.'

'It probably is a copy if you found it lying about the house. Clio keeps all our original documents in a file. For safety. Like our passports. She won't send them out in the post or anything.'

'I didn't find it lying about the house. I found it in my file at school. It must have got left there by mistake.'

And with this, he pulled a crumpled brown envelope from his back pocket. He pulled me aside, crouched down and spread it out across his thigh.

'There.'

It was clearly marked 'copy'. But I couldn't see the problem. His parents' names were there – or at least a Mr and Mrs Cassidy, née Kealey.

'It's the date,' he hissed, exasperated. 'I was born on the 23rd of May, 1995. This is dated 1999. Four years later,' he added, in case I proved to be remedially slow.

'No, it's not, there's your date of birth, there –'

'The *issue* date. It was *issued* in 1999. When I was nearly *four*. When I was starting Montessori.'

'And?'

'And where's the original?'

This was starting to smack of either fantasy or paranoia. But I could see from his face that he believed his own story.

'If your parents have any sense, like mine, they'll have put the original one in a safe place. Like I told you,' I reasoned. 'So they got a copy to hand in to your school? So what? Their names are on it. That's your mum, isn't it?

Susan Anne Cassidy, née Kealey. And your dad, Patrick Joseph Cassidy?'

'Yes. But why the four-year gap?'

It was clearly a rhetorical question.

'Because I'm adopted!' he crowed triumphantly. 'The original one will have my birth parents' names on it. My birth mother, anyway. And I can't see it till I'm eighteen. That's another seven months. In a way I'm glad,' he went on, 'because it makes sense of everything. Like I said.'

'Like?' I ventured.

'Like how we really don't have very much in common. They're so … staid. It's hard to describe. They're very reserved people. Always a bit in awe of authority. They don't like to rock the boat. They're always scared of what the neighbours will think. Y'know?'

Unlike the fearless free spirit crouched beside me?

'So why haven't you asked them?'

'I have. I asked my mum.'

'And what did she say?'

'She denied it. She would, wouldn't she? Since they'd kept it from me all my life. She just got all tearful and asked me not to upset my dad saying things like that.'

'That still doesn't make you adopted. Like I was saying, when I was nine –'

'I'm seventeen, Aimée. I know. I just know. In here. There's something not right about it all. And I won't be able to find out until I'm eighteen and get my hands on the original birth certificate. That's what's killing me.'

'What does Caoimhe think?'

'Then there's the JRA,' he dodges the question. 'You know, her arthritis. That's what they call it.'

'Don't muck me about. You told me it's not always hereditary. Or if it was, you wouldn't both necessarily get it. So that means nothing and you know it. As I said, what does Caoimhe think?'

He stretched himself to his full height and tucked the envelope back in his jeans pocket.

'She thinks I'm mad.'

I burst into involuntary laughter.

'Sorry, Darren. Sorry.'

'So you should be.'

But the corners of his mouth were twitching.

'She thinks I've got an overactive imagination and I'm making a mystery out of nothing.'

This seemed reasonable so I declined to demur.

'That's why this chance to come to Derry is so serendipitous,' he went on, earnestly. 'I think I have a connection with here.'

This was becoming more bizarre by the minute. I mean, I know everyone wants to be an adoptive Derrywan now, with the City of Culture and all; it's only natural, but ...

'Why?'

'Because I caught my mum out in a lie. And she never lies. When she was getting all excited about the Derry exchange, she told me it was a lovely city – even though she's never been here.'

'And?'

'And then a couple of nights later, after we'd had words, like, I heard her crying to my dad and she was talking about the time they brought me from Derry to the new house and how I was such a lovely baby and she'd never have thought it'd turn out like this ...'

'Did you ask her about it?'

'How could I? I only overheard it.'

I checked him. 'You were eavesdropping.'

'Well … OK. Eavesdropping.'

'Could you ask your aunties or uncles or grandparents or –'

He shook his head.

'All of my grandparents are dead. One auntie's in the States. The other two live across Dublin but it's not something you could just wade straight into with them. And they'd go straight to Mum and Dad. Even if you asked them not to.'

It was a blatant bid for sympathy. But I am Clio and Eamonn's daughter. They do not deal in sentimental mawkishness. Some would say Clio is downright cynical; she would argue that experience has made her so. Remember, I was the first in my class to know about the tooth fairy. And Santa being the Spirit of Christmas. Big and grown-up as the lad beside me might be, there was the echo of a lost and wistful child in his imagined circumstances of his birth. Time to confront it.

'And what do you want us to do?'

'Nothing, really. Just help me to get out and about here, look into people's faces –'

'And if anyone looks like a long-lost relative, you rush up and introduce yourself? Wise the bap, Darren; like I said before, the way people here go out at Hallowe'en their own mothers wouldn't recognise them. Adoptive or otherwise,' I added and immediately regretted it.

But information is strength and all Darren had was speculation. Make that a mad fantasy. Not a fact in it.

Time to consult Clio. And change the subject before he became completely self-obsessed. We switched the conversation to trivia. But not before Darren Cassidy had thanked me for being a good listener.

Me. Aimée Logan. Aka Motormouth.

'Not like your friend. Forgive me for saying it,' he added.

'Not at all!' I squealed.

'I mean, Bree, she's lovely –'

Like I don't know it?

'– but she's a bit weird, like, you know. She was *staring* at me the whole time I was trying to answer her question about JRA and I just knew she wasn't listening to a word I said. It was like she was undressing me with her eyes.'

He laughed. And I had the courage to laugh back.

'No "like" about it; she *was*. That's our Bree. You're safe enough though. She thinks she's found The One.'

I didn't bother to add that she was well on her way to losing him again. Why make trouble?

All too soon we were back at 1A Riverview.

'Here we are. I'm starving.'

I got out my key.

'Shame, in a way, though, Aimée. I could talk to you all night.'

The Mammy muttered a bit about whether we had long to wait for the order to be made up but I reminded her that microwaves are a wonderful invention. Just as well, as Rebekah's share was too much even for the four-legged eating machine. And no, she didn't call in. She just texted that she'd meet us at the school at five. No explanation.

Hey ho for Hallowe'en,
Lots of witches to be seen,
Some are pink, some are green,
Hey ho for Hallowe'en.

Forgive me a little regression therapy but what better time to unleash one's inner child than a Derry Hallowe'en? Considering some of the behaviour one could expect to witness over the next few hours, that was a relatively small aberration.

Our assembly point was at the playing field at half past five sharp (not Derry half past five, which is any time around six). There would be 'refreshments' followed by entertainment (Bree's Babes, the 8R Line dancers and Carly Jenkins's younger brother Blaine playing – yes – 'Danny Boy' on the flute) and then straight on to the coach to the parade start-point by the river.

I left Caoimhe and Darren in the safe if tediously boring hands of call-me-Nick's evaluation group. Fortified by the latest batch from an apparently never-ending supply of scones, I went to assemble the Babes.

Bree was in great good spirits. La Mooney, she informed me, was pig sick that (a) I had been allocated Darren and (b) her twin, whose father and mother both 'worked in broadcasting and film', had turned out to be the totally grounded daughter of an RTÉ rigger driver and a best boy (not sure which was which) who took great delight in (1) deconstructing the Mooneys' dream of their daughter being 'discovered', (2) pointing out it was all their own pretentious fault and (3) telling all her Knockgorey mates about it and how funny it was.

La Mooney does not like being the object of ridicule. And then there was me. I had been allocated Darren and seen walking the town with him, deep in conversation. (Yesss. Result.)

Such was my bonhomie that I agreed to let Bree introduce the Babes with her joke about choosing the Springsteen track partly because the troupe were all born in the USA – Up Stairs Altnagelvin (hospital, maternity unit).

Maybe it's mildly amusing if you haven't grown up with it.

Bree's Babes, while not 'babe-licious' as some nerd would later report in the school magazine, were, if I may say so as manager, surprisingly coordinated.

To be honest, I found it impossible to do a value judgement on the high kicking ministrations of our little troupe. It was too frustrating, watching Rebekah, Hannah and Rachael prancing in sisterly synchronisation and not being able to find out what was going on – with Tom, not Darren.

Not that I'm nosy or anything. I admit to an enquiring mind and a healthy interest in the affairs of my fellow students, that's all.

My first chance to get a discreet word with Rebekah came during Blaine Jenkins's solo.

'There's a chicken in lemon sauce with fried rice with your name on it in our kitchen.' I was trying to strike up a casual dialogue but she was clearly preoccupied with matters more serious.

'That was kind of your mum.'

'You didn't make it over this afternoon.'

'I never said I would.'

'Were you at Tom's?'

'Aimée!' She swung to face me. 'If I tell you what's going on will you swear – I mean *really* swear – not to tell Bree? She doesn't understand and she means well, but ... and it's Tom's business, not mine. In fact, all you really need to know,' she added curtly, 'is that his mum's in hospital but she's getting better. It's the best place for her at the minute. And Bree's Babes performed as expected and Tom and I will be on the Columban float. Then we're taking Rachael and Griffin up the town for a while – Rachael's allowed to go this year – and that's it. Tom and Griffin will be staying at their dad's for a couple of weeks,' she added, 'not that it's any of your business, Aimée.'

Before I could protest, I saw the tears welling in her eyes. And how totally exhausted she looked. Worse than 4 a.m.-feed tired.

'It's a big step for Tom,' she added, quietly, 'being able to trust someone. He likes to keep things private. It's a way of keeping his home life and his school life separate, I suppose. But he trusts you, Aimée, because he knows Clio knows his mum and knows about ... her problems.'

It was the longest speech I'd heard her make for weeks.

'So, back off, please, friend?'

What could I say? Or do? Am I really that nosy?

'And,' she added firmly, 'we have precisely nine minutes to change into costume. Or miss the coach.'

Rachael had been granted a leave of absence by the rest of the von Trapp O'Haras with a promise that she could stay out late with us provided we met up again at the family meeting point when the parade was over. Tom told us his dad had promised to meet them there with Griffin around 8.30 p.m., after the fireworks.

Mizz herded us onto the coach to be reunited with our painted backdrop.

*

'This is just amazing!'

Forget sophistication. Both Caoimhe and Darren were enchanted. No other description could suffice. It is a spectacle for all but the most claustrophobic to enjoy. And the float gave us a good vantage point.

By half past six, the streets were thronged with what the official literature refers to as 'colourful characters'. Sounds of Irish traditional, country 'n' Irish, chart covers and the unmistakable ta'i chi soundtrack sounded out from various stages and performance areas. Stilt-walkers and unicyclists tottered and wavered through the crowds. I reckoned this must be the only city in Western Europe, possibly the world, where a good seventy-five per cent of primary school kids are skilled in the diabolo and well versed in juggling.

The air was filled with the aroma of stale cooking oil, burnt sugar and, very possibly, weed. Stewards and marshals in fluorescent waistcoats vied with hearts-and-minds friendly police officers to confiscate alcohol from the underage, the inebriated, the street drinkers and the unwary. The occasional minor local celeb – a footballer, a television talent show veteran, a city councillor or a Rose of Tralee – smiled and waved and tried to be papped. Face-painters, balloon-modellers and buskers plied their trade, often free of charge; shops and stalls sold bobbing headbands and masks, light-up badges and glo-sticks in their hundreds.

'This is the family-friendly bit,' I warned them as they commented, yet again, on how everyone, regardless of age, gender, sexual orientation or ethnic origin, took part with enthusiasm. Anyone in civilian clothing was, quite honestly, a bit suspect. It would have been churlish of me to labour the point that no matter how vigilant the guardians of our peace and upholders of our civic pride, by the early hours of the morning it would not be unusual to see Pudsey Bear knocking ten bells out of Fred Flintstone in a taxi queue, nor a bevy of nuns being evicted at speed from a nightclub.

We got away with waving at Gran – I must apologise to her for underestimating the size of the crowd, which included a few randomers who joined in the sequence, uninvited. T'ai chi clearly has its own well-defined fan base.

*

'I *so* enjoyed that.'

Caoimhe and I had found what might euphemistically be described as a 'quiet spot' in the family-friendly zone to cast our critical eye over the rest of the proceedings.

'You don't mind me using the chair? Really, Aimée? Cause I could always go back to your place –'

'Don't be stupid.'

I suspected Caoimhe was in more pain than she was going to admit to. I'd seen her surreptitiously swallowing a couple of paracetamol.

'But you might want to try to get in somewhere ...'

'No way.' I meant it, too.

It was such fun people-watching and slagging off their costumes that I didn't envy Bree and the gangsters their half-hearted trek round the clubs and pubs as they tried to coerce a door consultant into accepting their fake ID in exchange for the seasonally exorbitant cover charge.

As the smaller kiddies were trailed home, some only a few years older were congregating outside the offies or around the walls.

I eavesdropped shamelessly as Caoimhe took a call on her mobile and assured her parents that (1) she was having a great time, (2) it was a bad line and (3) she was taking it easy and we would be home soon. The levels of background noise suggested that (2) was true and (3) was patently false, but all parties seemed content with the deception. Clio and Eamonn always said I only got my current level of independence because I was responsible; a phrase which, like 'reliable', does not sit easily with an almost-sixteen-year-old. But I made a mental note to thank them for not being overprotective.

'I'm off then. Catch you later.'

Caoimhe showed no surprise as Darren, still clad in his Celtic cloak, vanished into the crowd.

'Where's he gone?'

'He'll be grand. Come on, Aimée, we can hardly expect him to spend a night like this babysitting two fifteen-year-old girls, can we? He's desperate to check out the talent. Your mam won't mind, will she? I told him I'd kill him if he wasn't back by ten,' she went on, oblivious to the devastation to my ego. 'At the latest. Half nine, ideally. That's when Rebekah and Tom and the younger ones are due back here, isn't it?'

'And my mother has booked a taxi driver she knows for ten sharp. We can't leave him waiting round cause of the night it is ...'

'Aimée ... I hope you don't mind me bringing this up, y'know?'

What? That it was blatantly obvious that, defying all logic, I had a massive crush on your brother? And if he rejoined us with a female appendage in a skimpy costume I would be outwardly vibrant and inwardly gutted?

'Bringing what up?'

'I know he's been bending your ear with his poor little orphan bit. What do you make of it?'

'What do *you*?' I batted back the question.

'You know what I think. Darren will have told you. Don't even try to deny it.'

'OK. Point taken. It's very straightforward to me.' I realised it was true as I said it. 'Why doesn't he just ask? And keep asking till he gets an answer? It'd be far better than this –'

Caoimhe shook her head.

'It's not that easy. No, really. I can't explain it and you won't understand until you come and visit us – you have to – but I could never talk to my mum like you talk to yours. She's lovely, she's so good to us and all; Darren doesn't appreciate her and I'm always getting on to him about it. But it's just different. We don't talk about things like that. You talk about everything.'

I took it as a compliment.

'You're so ... natural about everything. Like my wheels. It's so much better than being well-meaning. Now I'm embarrassed,' she smiled, shyly.

Time to come clean.

'I never even thought about it until you arrived,' I said.

Then I explained. About the green pages and Bree's thighs and the cryptic remarks and the Da and his newspaper feature, and we laughed and laughed so much that we almost didn't mind when it started to drizzle.

We were just getting to the chilly and shivery and fed-up stage when Caoimhe saw Rebekah and Tom running towards us with Griffin in tow. But no Rachael von Trapp.

Rebekah was shouting something incomprehensible. Then an ambulance drove past us. Up towards the bridge. At speed. Blue lights flashing. Two police cars passed it going the other way towards the river. The pub across the road disgorged a pile of rowdy and foul-mouthed drunks. The mood changed in an instant. Time to go.

I could make out what Beks was saying, now. 'Have you seen Rachael?'

Then Tom, straining to be heard over the hubbub, adding, 'She went to look for you two.'

Caoimhe looked up from her mobile. 'Darren's switched his phone off. He promised he wouldn't.'

Mine buzzed.

'Maybe this is him calling.'

But the phone was flashing Bree. Though it didn't sound like Bree. Not even a loved-up or mildly silly, tiddly Bree. Just a whisper, very young and very frightened.

'Aimée? Aimée, can you get Clio? Aimée, we're being arrested ...'

And her phone cut out.

And I heard Caoimhe calling, 'Aimée, that's our taxi. For Logan, yeah? That's us.'

And the heavens opened.

'What'll I do?' This from Caoimhe. 'You said he won't be able to wait ...' She sounded anxious.

I tried to think straight. But for once, I couldn't.

Chapter
Fourteen

W hat I wanted to do was throw the biggest tantrum since I was three. I remember, it was one of the very few times that both my parents said 'no' to me. They *never* did that, either separately or in unison. All I wanted was to take home the six foot tall fibre-optic snowman. Not much for a toddler to ask.

But I digress. Disasters were compounding. I needed time to think. I needed the Mammy. Three pairs of anxious eyes were looking at me in the hope that I, good old Aimée, had a list, a plan, a strategy, a coping mechanism.

I didn't.

'Hang on to that taxi!' I advised. Possession is nine-tenths of the law, right? And at least we'd have wheels. And that rain was down for the night, by the looks of it.

'Get in,' I shouted at Rebekah as Tom helped Caoimhe into the back seat and the driver folded up her chair. I pushed Griffin in after her. He was incongruously dressed as a pixie. A bloody big pixie, I might add.

'But we can't leave Rachael!' Rebekah was positively wailing.

'We won't find her by hanging around here.'

'But she'll be on her way back here.'

Tom made the decision by pushing Rebekah in after Griffin and I just had time to whisper in her ear as I hopped in, 'Bree's been arrested,' before the driver turned the vehicle in the general direction of the bridge.

'Wait a minute, can we just drive round for a bit?' That was Rebekah again, still distraught.

The driver looked in his mirror. 'I take it you're joking?'

'We're looking out for someone.'

'In this traffic? I rest my case.'

At that point an undisciplined throng of sailors underlined the wisdom of the driver's words as they began tugging at the taxi's handles and banging on its roof. Not an attempted hijacking, I assured my Dublin twin, just men in need of a lift home, strong coffee, Berocca and a change of clothing.

'But my sister's out there, lost, and she's only eleven ...' Rebekah's wail was only partly smothered by Tom's cloaked shoulder.

Had the driver no compassion? Had she no sense? Had I any ideas?

The driver stated his case: 'We're booked for Riverview Apartments. McCourt, right? That your mother?'

'Mine,' I said.

'Works at the uni? Does a bit at the women's centre too?'

So much for confidentiality. 'That's her.'

'Aye, I always lift her, so I do. She rang to check I was collecting yous. Lovely woman, your mother.'

Light-bulb moment. Mother, and probably Jilly, were back in Riverview. Phone home.

'Clio?'

'Did the taxi not turn up? I checked with them; they promised it would be a seven seater; they said the driver had dropped off Jilly and was on his way across town. I'll ring them –'

'No, Mammy, we're *in* it. Caoimhe and Rebekah and Tom and Griffin and me. We're heading home,' I added unnecessarily, trying to drown out Beks's squeals of 'Tell her about Rachael.'

'We've a bit of a problem,' I continued, 'Rachael's missing. Well, not *missing*, but we're not sure where she is.'

'And where's Darren?'

I looked at Caoimhe.

'We're not sure about that either. But it's OK, Caoimhe rang home so Mr and Mrs Cassidy know they're fine. Bree's been arrested,' I added unhelpfully. 'Mam, what'll we do?'

'OK, OK,' Clio said soothingly, 'just get home and we'll figure this out.'

*

Clio was at the front door, looking out for us, cash in hand, which was just as well – I'd probably have forgotten all about paying the driver, never mind that it was undoubtedly fare-and-a half tonight. She had our old papier mâché false face over the porch light (How did she climb up there? Wind assisted?) and a pumpkin lantern in the front window. Inside, the kitchen counter was laden with a spread to satisfy the most mendicant trick-or-treaters, everything from sugar slugs and mini lollies to individual bags of Monster Munch. The air was warm with apple pie spice. Candles? No, definitely oven: there was whipped cream.

I hoped she'd had at least a few trick-or-treaters. She gets upset if she doesn't and there aren't many small children round our apartments; it's mostly singles and what she says used to be called dinkys in her day (double income, no kids yet).

It was so good to be home. A real regression moment. Why did I have to grow old enough to go up the town? I could have sat here all night, eating home-made apple tart and winning at Articulate. And we have what the council calls a 'panoramic vista' of the fireworks display from our lounge window. Up the town, you don't really get to see them (unless you crane your neck backwards at a painful angle and gaze at the heavens).

'List, Aimée.'

Not, What happened? Why? Who? Just 'list'.

'Help yourselves,' Clio said as Griffin dug in. 'And put on the telly. The fireworks might be on the local news at half past ten. You might see yourselves.'

I quickly took out a couple of pens and a clean sheet of paper.

1

Rachael. Mobile? O'Haras? Family liaison point?

2

Darren. Mobile? Caoimhe any idea? (Over sixteen.)

My mother looked over my shoulder as I wrote and grabbed her own pen. Slowly, I began to feel a little better and more sure. Amazing things, lists are.

3

Bree arrested.

Clio's expression was quizzical.
'With GoPual's lot,' I elaborated.
'Do you know that for sure, Aimée?'
'No. But she rang me .... and now her phone's dead ...'
Clio leaned over and wrote:

4

Police. Eamonn. Volunteers, civic wardens. Teams. Drinkwatch, security.

'Eamonn might still be in the office and reporters always know what's going on.'

At this point she began removing items of costume, starting with the wig. I remembered that she'd had plans of her own.

'Where's Jilly?' I asked.

'Not on your missing persons list, thankfully.' Mam smiled. 'It's all right. She got a better offer. I was staying in with Rainbow anyway,' Mam added. 'I closed him in but he's nervous on his own. He only likes loud noises if he's involved in making them. And your gran is at home now, too; she rang earlier.'

Wig, earrings, torque and bangles removed, Mam assumed full-on counsellor mode with such a vigour that I suspected she might actually be enjoying it a bit.

'Caoimhe,' she said, 'if you know anything about what Darren's up to, I really think you should tell us. Otherwise, he's seventeen, he can look after himself.'

This notion seemed to amuse his sister.

'You can keep trying his phone,' Clio went on. 'I'm sure we're worrying about nothing. He knew what time the taxi was ordered for and he knows our address. He'll find his own way home. Don't worry,' she added, less brusquely, seeing Caoimhe's face starting to look worried.

'Now, Rebekah, tell me about Rachael.'

'She was allowed up the town with us for an hour. After the parade. She just got separated from us. And we thought maybe she'd tried to find her way to Aimée at the liaison point. That's what she was supposed to do if she got lost.'

'And how many liaison points are there?' my mother asked, though it was clear that she knew the answer.

'I thought there was one, but ...'

'*Three*,' she said firmly. 'Check the civic programme. There should be a helpline number on the back.' She handed it to Beks along with the cordless phone. 'Go on, you ring it. You can describe her best. She's your sister.'

Then she picked up her mobile. Clearing a space on the kitchen table, aka central control, she reached for her notebook and pen.

'Eamonn. No, Aimée is fine. She's here. Why? Is there bother up the town? That's why I was ringing, actually. I'm just looking for a wee bit of off-the-record info. What do you know about any arrests?'

Across the room, Beks was giving us a thumbs-up sign and Tom was hugging her – a little too enthusiastically for mixed company, in my opinion.

I tried to listen in to both calls simultaneously but then I heard Caoimhe's mobile ringing. 'Darren? Where are you?'

'Have you got Sorcha's number?' Mam was hissing at me, while still writing in her own form of shorthand (which is as indecipherable to the casual observer as to the trained encrypter, for all she slags off Mizz Hardy's efforts). She was making encouraging noises down the phone to elicit the maximum amount of news.

I rang Sorcha. It was on answerphone. She'd be up the town. Of course. Everyone was.

'Right.'

Mam hung up the phone.

'Did you get her?'

I shook my head. 'She's switched off.'

'That means no one will be able to get her. So,' Clio continued, 'we may have to sort out the Bree situation. Now, what about Rachael?'

Found, Beks told us. At an alternative family liaison point. Tearful, wet and fed-up standing and looking out for her sister. But safe. A civic warden would deliver her to us in the next batch of displaced youngsters.

'Ring your family,' my mother urged Rebekah, 'and say she's over with us. That'll stop them worrying.'

'They won't be worried,' Rebekah reasoned. 'They think she's with me. And she will be. Soon.'

'Right. Good thinking. And Darren?'

'Much the same. Apart from the tearful bit,' Caoimhe assured us. 'He's had a great time. His battery was low and he switched off his phone for a while to save it. He's in a queue at a taxi rank near the Guildhall. He's nineteenth in line.'

'We'll see him tomorrow, then,' I muttered ungraciously.

Clio ignored this. 'Now, Aimée, what exactly do you know about Bree? This is important. Eamonn says there have been the usual arrests for disorderly behaviour and drink-related offences and that. He says the police have been picking up underage drunks all evening. They take their alcohol off them and then take them home in a Land Rover. If there's an adult at home, they give the child a caution in front of them.'

'That wouldn't be like Bree,' I interrupted.

'There have also been a few arrests for drug-related offences.'

That wouldn't be like Bree either, but

Clio and I exchange looks. Neither of us says anything.

There is nothing worse than labelling people because of where they live. Mam would kill me for doing it. But the Sycamore Heights crowd? Eamonn reckons the entire estate should be helping the PSNI with their enquiries. We all know the joke: What do you call a young fella from Sycamore Heights wearing a suit? The defendant.

'We last saw her before we went off to join the float,' Rebekah offered. 'She was going home to change into her costume and then she was going up the town to meet Paul and them.'

'She rang me,' I said miserably. 'That was when we were getting into the taxi so, say, just coming up to ten. She just shouted that she was being arrested and then her phone went dead.'

'Or someone took it off her.' Clio lifted the phone. 'If she has been arrested – and I say *if* – the police will have been trying to get Sorcha. Willie's next-of-kin too, of course, but he's outside the jurisdiction ...'

'And anyway, he never answers the phone,' I added.

'Custody sergeant, please,' Clio demanded briskly. 'Hello? Yes. This is Clio McCourt from the Department of Gender Studies at Magee. Hello. I wonder if you can help me. I do some volunteer work with a number of youth groups ... yes, that's right, yes, the teenage mums ... Yes, I know Sergeant Nixon, that's right. I'll tell you why I'm ringing ...'

'Watch the expert at work.' I nudge Caoimhe.

The doorbell rings.

A very wet and weepy Rachael von Trapp. A very angry Rachael von Trapp. Who rounded on her elder sister.

'You *lost* me. You and *him*.' She jabbed a small accusing finger at Tom. 'You were too busy eating the faces off each other.' She pointed at Griffin, who was half asleep on the sofa. 'And it's his fault too. He never talked to me or anything.'

'You ran off,' Rebekah suggests.

'I did not. I was only having a look round so I could tell my friends all about it because they weren't allowed out on their own.' She started to gulp. 'And I was having the best day ever cause I was a Bree's Babe and now it's ruined and I think I might be pregnant.'

She started to howl and ran out into the hall, slamming the door behind her. Rebekah jumped up and ran after her. Caoimhe shouted, 'What happened, pet, what happened?' and Clio signalled for us all to pipe down as she was clearly getting someone's charge sheet in detail from her PSNI source.

As we sat, stunned, the door opened again, just a fraction, and a small tear-stained face reappeared to add, 'And if I am pregnant, it was a cow that did it!'

Chapter Fifteen

ust when I thought it couldn't get any worse, the doorbell rang. Darren, swathed in wet hessian and smelling like a farmyard.

'I walked,' he said brightly, by way of explanation. 'I got talking to these two nurses. Well, they weren't nurses but, you know, they were dressed as nurses, in skimpy little uniforms and suspenders and stilettos –'

Too. Much. Detail.

' – and we decided to leg it over. The taxis were taking forever and people were queue-jumping like mad. It was getting rowdy,' he added, heading straight for the kitchen. 'The girls were a bit worried about walking over the bridge but I said I'd look after them.'

I'm sure you did. 'Make yourself at home,' I said drily as Darren switched on the kettle and slid a huge slice of Clio's apple tart on to a plate. 'How did you find the way?'

'This is excellent.' He paused between shovelfuls. 'I've a fairly good sense of direction and I had the address. The girls knew Riverview. They're in the apartments down near the railway station.'

'That's miles away. In the opposite direction,' I pointed out.

'Are the rest of them in the living room?' Darren went on, oblivious to my steely look. 'I can't wait to tell them. Come on Aimée, you're not sore at me, are you? I mean, how could you be in the European Capital of Hallowe'en and not get to go round town a bit?'

'Have you been drinking?' I asked primly.

'A couple of cans. The girls gave them to me. They were eighteen. They thought I was eighteen or nineteen,' he added unnecessarily. 'Hey, Aimée – chill. It's a couple of beers, OK? I wasn't trying to buy it with false ID or anything stupid, not like I bet that daft friend of yours does … Hey, what's up?'

To my disgust, tears were streaming down my face. Maybe I was just overtired.

'Bree's been arrested,' I choked. 'And we lost Rachael. And you. And Rachael thinks she's pregnant and she's out in the bedroom with Rebekah now, but she can't be cause she's talking crap about it being a cow.'

'Hey, steady, steady.' Darren pulled me close to the wet, scratchy, smelly cloak. It felt great.

The door opened. 'Aimée, I need – pardon *me*,' and Beks shut the door in a nanosecond and retreated back into the bedroom.

'Beks – it's not –' I shouted as Darren and I leapt apart. (OK, he leapt apart from me.)

The doorbell. Again. Trick-or-treaters at this hour? Surely not. No, it was the Da, minus the Cute Lensman and/or any form of loot bag.

'Where's your mam?'

'On the phone.' I indicated the living room. 'To the police. Bree's been –'

'I know. That's why I'm here. I wanted to make sure it was her and then I came over to drive your mam to the police station to get her out.'

In the living room, I took in a sleeping heap of Griffin, Tom, Caoimhe and Rainbow. Not all together but you get the picture. I gathered it had been a long twenty-four hours for all of them. Emotional stress can be very tiring.

'Sorcha can't be found.' That was the Da.

'We know,' I said.

'It's not a problem. She'll be up the town and probably not in a fit state to go to the custody suite. We can sort it ourselves.'

I was impressed.

'Right, Clio, are you ready?'

'Just getting my bag. I don't think Bree has been charged with anything, Eamonn, not from what I can find out, but she has to stay there until a responsible adult collects her.'

That could be a problem, I mused, cynically but silently. Mind you, my own contemporaries hadn't exactly been role models of sober common sense either.

'Aimée, have you any idea who Sorcha's solicitor is? I should really leave a message with them.'

I shrugged. Even when she's not wearing her Human Rights Activist hat, Mam refuses to accept that I was one of only a very few kids in reception class who could reel off their name, address, date of birth and solicitor. Apart from the totally career-criminal families. Still, it did my street cred no harm at all.

'We can sort this out once we get there. Or tomorrow.' Clio was firm. 'But Eamonn, we're only going to sign for Bree. I don't know the others, I only know of them.'

My mother 'knows of' a lot of people through her various areas of work, both paid and voluntary.

'Thanks. Really, thanks, Eamonn. It's more than good of you.'

'I knew you'd no chance of getting a taxi,' he replied gruffly.

The Da? Embarrassed?

'Tell me about it. I had to walk over the bridge and back,' offered the wet one, aka Darren Cassidy.

'You had two nurses to look after you,' I remarked, a comment which went ignored.

'And what's this about Rachael? I take it she's scared herself stupid but it's a load of nonsense? Really, Mrs O'Hara should make sure those girls know the basic facts. But then again … anyway, Aimée, I can rely on you to look after that, can't I? Your dad might take them home later?'

The Da nodded in resigned acceptance. 'I'm on duty anyway,' he said. 'I won't be partying. And there'll be a special court in the morning. There always is after a big event,' he added by way of explanation to Darren, forgetting that he is a Dub, not an innocent abroad.

A small, bedraggled von Trapp slunk into the living room, cheeks blazing. 'I'm so sorry Mrs – Ms McCourt. I didn't mean to be a bother. I was being really silly. I just got scared. And I *am* trained to cope in an emergency,' she glared at her big sister, 'and I did what I knew I should do. I borrowed a phone and rang the emergency services but I couldn't get through.'

'But you have to get put through, even if there's no credit on the phone,' my mother reasoned. 'Maybe you were frightened and didn't dial properly?'

'I did,' the small one was definite. 'I dialled 911, like you're supposed to.'

'Like it tells you on TV?' I suggested, as Eamonn hustled a chuckling Clio out the door. 'Rachael, it's 999 in this country,' I explained. '911 is only in America.'

Separated parents departed, I was now officially head of the household. Time to take charge.

1

Get Rachael out of wet clothes.
Borrow some of Caoimhe's.

2

Get Darren out of wet clothes. Has he spares?
Borrow mine? Please, God, let us not be the
same jeans size.

3

Tumble dryer on, tidy up kitchen, clear leftover food, but first,

4

Find out what really happened to Rachael.

It's the journalistic genes in me. I am *not* nosy. We established that, way back.

'Oh my goodness, I am so sorry. I didn't mean to doze off. Darren. You're back!' Caoimhe looked truly happy.

'He came home under medical escort,' I assured her. 'Part of the way, at least.'

'And Rachael, how are you, pet?'

And that was when we heard the whole sorry tale. The jury is still out on whether Tom and Beks were in fact 'eating the faces off each other', as Rachael had so delicately put it, or whether the eleven-year-old had seen an opportunity for flight and then lost her family, her friends and her common sense.

It seemed a crowd of Castle Grove Year 9s, aka Old McDonald's Farm, had set up home on a bench by the river and invited her over to join them. In the ensuing frolics, a randy youth in a bovine costume had pulled Miss von Trapp onto his knee in a knobbly embrace. The unfortunate Rachael sat on something hard and penetrating and feared the worst.

A plastic udder had a lot to answer for, but not a pregnancy scare.

I saw Caoimhe glaring at Darren, willing him not to burst out laughing. He muttered something about making coffee and ran for the kitchen before he exploded into giggles.

'I'll give you a hand,' Tom volunteered.

This is *my* kitchen, right?

'We'll clear up for your mam, too,' he added. 'She's been really sound.'

Left to our own devices, we girlies discussed costumes, both good (our float) and gross (Simon C-K as a shower curtain, of all things. Talk about attention-seeking. Beks said he kept inviting young women to see what he was wearing under it and I said he was lucky he wasn't in the police station with Bree on a charge of gross indecency.) This of course defeated the purpose of the small talk which was to keep everyone from thinking about Bree, which we all were anyway. Well, Beks and I were and probably Caoimhe. Rachael and Griffin were asleep in front of some horror film that was patently unsuitable for their age group.

I fed Caoimhe with enough detail to slag off her brother about his escorts and she went into their room (my room) to get him dry jeans and a T-shirt.

'I'll help,' I offered, ever the perfect hostess, sneaking a look at the label on his jeans. Thirty-two inches. Thank God. I have never ever been more than a thirty. Honestly. And Bree's twenty-four is unnatural. Isn't it? For a human?

Once the wet clothing was in the dryer and the dishes were done, the party gravitated into the kitchen where, it seemed, Darren and Tom had struck up quite a rapport in a short time. Maybe Beks was right – maybe Tom was really easy to talk to. Or maybe it was the universal language of soccer and computer games.

Caoimhe interrupted their discussion to probe her brother on whether he had really been out and about taking in the sights or if there was another reason for his momentary disappearance.

'You've been very down,' Caoimhe ventured. 'Or very devious. You don't know how worried I've been about you. And so have Mum and Dad.'

'Are you glad you came to Derry?' This was Tom.

Darren looked round the room. 'With a night like this and good friends around me? I'd be mad to say no. And then, tomorrow –'

I had almost forgotten about that.

'What's tomorrow?' Tom asked. 'Apart from a day off school?'

'Tomorrow Eamonn is very kindly driving us out into Donegal. To do some sightseeing. How many of us could he fit into his car, Aimée?'

Presumptuous or what?

'I couldn't go, thanks all the same,' Beks said quickly. 'I've had my Hallowe'en. I'm on babysitting duty. Wee Jacob's so cute,' she added, lest we detect begrudgery in her voice. 'He's no bother. He's a wee dote.'

Tom nodded earnestly.

'He is that.'

Perhaps after Griffin anyone would seem like a wee dote. But I wasn't too tired to register Tom's inclusion in the O'Haras' domestic routine. Neither Bree nor I had been invited to spend more than a token amount of quality time with the latest addition to the family.

'Count me out, too, thanks all the same,' said Tom. 'I'll be keeping her company. And I'll be keeping an eye out for Griffin. We'll be staying with my dad for maybe a week, if it's the usual form.'

'Look on the bright side,' smiled Beks. 'KFC buckets seven nights in a row.'

I cringed for Clio, in absentia.

There was an embarrassed silence.

'But we must meet up before you go,' Tom urged Darren, 'if we can manage it. For a bit more craic.'

And we hugged a big, comfortable, group hug. And we held on for ages and ages until the phone and the doorbell rang at once. That's the way it always happens in 1A Riverview.

*

'Do you realise it's gone one in the morning?'

Eamonn was shaking his head as he helped the O'Haras, Tom and Griffin into the car.

'Past my bedtime you mean?' I tried (and failed) to raise one eyebrow.

'I'm just thinking maybe you should turn in. Clio told me to get this lot home and by the time I've done that she hopes she will be ready to leave. With Bree,' he added. 'And no, Aimée, I don't know what happened. All I know is the police are claiming they intercepted a big drug deal tonight and they're questioning what they say is "a number of teenagers". Serious stuff. But your mother is a force to be reckoned with. If – and I say *if* – Bree hasn't been charged with anything, Clio will take her back here with her. And if she is charged, we can stand bail and get on to our solicitor first thing tomorrow morning – I mean, this morning.'

'Are you two OK to go home?' I heard Rebekah ask, and Tom's quiet reply, 'I have a key. Dad will be out. Or in bed.'

'Your friend Bree is dafter than I thought, getting in-volved with that Sycamore Heights crowd,' my da muttered. 'I thought she'd have more sense. Not that you should label people –'

'I know, I know.' I nodded. 'I think she was giving it one last chance.' Guilty? Me? I felt like a total and utter bitch and worst friend ever. Poor, silly, lovely Bree. And it was, at least partly, my fault, encouraging her to give GoPual another chance, all to keep Darren to myself. How stupid, how childish can you get?

After they'd gone, the apartment seemed unnaturally quiet as we waited for news of Bree. Mercifully, none of us made any pathetic attempts at gallows humour.

'Tom seems really sound,' Caoimhe commented and we all agreed. 'And unlike some, he has something genuine to worry about.'

Darren looked bewildered.

'His mother's a mess, Darren.' Caoimhe was suddenly serious. 'Makes you realise … Mum and Dad are great, you know? OK, they're a bit overprotective –'

'*Very* overprotective.'

'OK, then, very overprotective. I laughed so much when you sent me that email about going out round the pubs and clubs of Dublin, Aimée. I hardly ever go into the city centre. I never get out the door. Well, that's not strictly true, but you know what I mean. I certainly don't have the freedom you have.'

'Maybe this will be a trial run for a bit more independence,' I suggested.

She smiled. 'Do you know, Aimée – please don't laugh at this – I've never even had a boyfriend! Not a proper one.'

Please don't ask me, I willed. Please don't ask me about my relationship history in front of Darren.

'And now,' she went on, 'if you'll excuse me, I really am going to get changed into my jammies and turn in. Mum and Dad would have a fit if they knew I was up this late! But promise – both of you, now – promise to wake me up as soon as you hear from Bree.'

'Promise,' I said, yawning.

'Do you want me to sit up with you?' Darren didn't look one bit tired. He looked like he could sit up all night. It would have been inhospitable to chase him off to his (my) room.

And wrecked though I was, I really couldn't sleep till I heard what was happening in the police station.

Rainbow unrolled himself and headed Caoimhe-wards. Darren and I sat in companionable silence for a while.

Then he said, 'Caoimhe's right, Aimée. You're very natural with people. Like your mum.'

Natural sounds better than organised, doesn't it?

'Caoimhe told me about the missing paperwork,' he said with a grin. 'You have no idea. Mum and Dad would *so* not have let her come to Derry if they didn't think you and Clio had taken an intensive course in disability awareness.'

'OK,' I muttered, embarrassed.

'I've promised her I'll try to get her out more when we go back,' he went on. 'And I've promised her something else. That I'll try to stop all this crap and be a bit less of a pain round the house. Not that I'm that bad. And what about you, Aimée? What are you promising yourself?'

'That's easy.' I warmed to my favourite topic. 'I am so fed up with being organised and sensible and level-headed and dependable and hard-working and all those things. Do you know, I am a legend for list-making? I'm fifteen!'

He laughed again, that lovely, mellow laugh of his.

'No,' I went on, 'if I had a fairy godmother with a magic wand, or the power of reincarnation, neither of which I believe in, incidentally, I'd come back as a fluffy airhead. And totally gorgeous with it.'

The silence hung between us. I felt myself cringe. Whywhywhy did I say that? Can I laugh it off, backtrack in some way, say it was a joke? A bad joke?

'You really mean that, don't you?' Darren looked straight into my eyes.

'No, not at all. Well, yes, to be honest. I'd love to be more like Bree. Not getting arrested and getting groped by GoPual, of course. But gorgeous and lively and popular and able to charm the birds off the bushes.'

'A man magnet you mean.'

'Yes.'

'Until you open your mouth.'

'What?'

'Bree is very lovely,' Darren said, with a remarkable degree of mature objectivity, 'but she's a mentalist. She's a liability. Look at tonight. Where would she be without you and your family? Her own mother isn't around to help out. I can say that to you – I'm not mouthing about her. But like you said, she's only fifteen. Take Sorcha – what I hear of her, anyway – and my mum. One extreme to the other. You wouldn't think they're from the same generation.'

'They might not be,' I mused. 'Sorcha's about thirty-six, maybe thirty-seven at the most.'

'My mum's over fifty. She's … fifty-five, nearly. Adoptive mothers often are that bit older …'

'She could be Sorcha's mother.'

That is scary.

Darren broke the silence. 'She's not the sharpest card in the pack,' he added. 'Bree.'

'She's not,' I agreed disloyally.

'How many of her homeworks have you done for her while she's out on the town? Come on, Aimée, I'm not daft. She's a lovely person. But let's just say she's at her most fanciable before she opens her mouth.'

'You're a bloke,' I muttered. 'You're not supposed to think like that. Bree's supposed to be irresistible.'

'Well, believe me, I can resist her. And that boyfriend of hers, GoPual, hardly seems like a catch.'

Darren had called him GoPual!

'Believe me, he's not,' I agreed happily.

We smiled at each other.

Emboldened, I went on. 'But it's easy for you to say that. You must know you're, well …' – and I put on a silly voice to mask my embarrassment – 'very attractive to the opposite sex.'

'Sure. And I look older than my age, too.'

'Cut the false modesty. Your picture caused quite a frisson in Castle Grove.'

'And what about in 1A Riverview, Aimée?'

Even in the dusk he must have seen my cheeks burning.

'I'm sorry. That was unfair.'

'You can get away with it,' I said, trying to sound offhand.

'Maybe. OK. It can be an advantage, some of the time. But it's a pain always being taken for a couple of years older than you are. Then when you won't go into offies for your friends or gatecrash 21s events they get fed up with you. And the girls who come on to you tend to be that bit older. Which is not always what you want. And – laugh all you like, it's true, Aimée – some of the girls you'd really like to get to know won't come near you because they think you'll be all cocky, and wouldn't look sideways at them, when the opposite is true. And some of the others treat you like … like …'

'An airhead?' I suggested.

'Yeah, an airhead. Arm candy.'

This time the laughter was companionable.

'You're great, Aimée, you know.'

'You said that before.'

'That's because I mean it.'

Neither of us heard the car pull up outside. I think we may have hugged for, oh, at least two minutes before I heard a screech: 'You will not believe –'

And Bree burst into the living room, my da's sweat-shirt covering what remained of gangsta sista's scanties.

'Oh,' she said as Darren jumped back in his seat. She gave me what I think is described as a searching look before returning to her favourite topic.

'Wait till I tell you what happened,' she began with theatrical flourish. 'It has been the worst night of my life, ever. And see Clio? She is a saint, and this man ...' By now she was playing to the gallery. Bree spun round but Eamonn had obviously decided discretion was the better part of valour and headed for the door. 'What can I say? See your dad, Aimée? He was pure magic. He knows a lot of policemen,' she observed.

'It's an occupational hazard for a journalist,' I muttered darkly.

'Hello, Clio,' Darren greeted my mother. 'I did promise Caoimhe we'd wake her up again when you got in. So I'd better.'

Reluctantly, I reverted to type. Reliable and dependable and well organised. I followed him out and went to put on the kettle for Clio's hot chocolate. A double. With a marshmallow on top. Four hours of unmitigated Bree? She clearly deserved it.

*

'So tell us.' Caoimhe, wrapped in a duvet, perched on the sofa, wide-eyed. 'What happened? Like, did they grab you and throw you in the back of the police van and drive off with the sirens going and the blue lights flashing?'

'Well, as I was saying to Clio, it's a long story.'

'We've got all night,' Darren prompted her. 'But stick to the facts, yeah? You don't need to be hyping it up. It's serious as it is.'

'Well, *I* haven't got all night. Or even all morning, to be precise.' Clio's tone was decisive. 'I'm away to bed. Aimée, are you and Bree going to sleep in here?'

I knew this was an instruction, not a suggestion.

I helped the Mammy carry the air bed and some spare sheets and quilts into the living-room. 'Don't let her lose the run of herself,' my mother whispered. 'She was terrified when I got to see her.'

'Why were they lifted? Bree's never done drugs.'

'It may all be a misunderstanding involving a pair of pinstriped trousers, would you believe. But they aren't too keen on letting the rest of them go.'

'Brendy? Paul?'

'And a few others. One of them slapped a policeman. Not the smartest move. And from what I can make out they were all fairly foul-mouthed. Not that it justifies arresting them but that's another matter. I'm getting someone from the Juvenile Law Commission to go up in the morning, especially if they're still holding the lads.'

'And Bree?'

'That should be the last she hears of it. She's not on bail or anything. But she has an official caution now and that gets recorded.'

'Jesus.'

'Exactly.'

Clio suddenly reached out and hugged me.

'And you've had it all to handle back here. You're a wee marvel.'

Another epithet for my collection.

'You'll enjoy the cow pregnancy story,' I assured her, woman-to-woman. 'It totally vindicates your theories on sex education.'

'*Mañana.*'

She rubbed her eyes and I realised she'd been working for the best part of twenty-four hours.

'Your dad will be here around noon. I told him there was no point in coming any earlier. You'll all be dead to the world. Then he's going to take you all for lunch before he goes back to work to photograph them leaving Castle Grove. He knows he has to have you back here to pack and be at the coach before six.'

'Doesn't time fly when you're enjoying yourself?' I'm not sure if I was being sarcastic or not. 'Night night, Mammy.'

*

Stripped of all drama, re-enactment and verbatim dialogue, Bree's was a sad and sorry story. By the time they reached the town, Carly had had a huge row with Brendy because he was (a) half-cut, (b) stoned and (c) aggressive, and she had gone off to try to meet up with her sister and her mates. That left Bree with seven or eight fellas, not all of whom she knew and some of whom she definitely didn't want to know. Vodka was passed round, substances may or may not have been taken and as the male party became increasingly loud-mouthed and rough, life started to imitate art for the gangsta gang. They were walking back towards Sycamore Heights to meet other friends-of-friends, amid much mobile phoning and texting, when Brendy and a couple of others started to slag off Paul for having a 'posh' girl with him. (This seemed to offend Bree more than anything.)

Someone decided to de-bag him (how mature) and his gangsta pinstripes were thrown over the telephone wire across the street, leaving him effing and blinding in his Homer Simpson underbags.

'De-bag him? Sounds like they took his take-away off him!' This from Caoimhe.

Another one for my planned cross-border cross-community phrasebook.

'Is that a Derryism?' she persisted.

'It's English public school slang,' I advised. 'Removal of trousers for purposes of alleged humour.'

'It wasn't funny,' Bree insisted. 'Well, not at the time.'

Next thing the police swooped, not because GoPual was causing an affront to public decency but because some keen-eyed wannabe detective inspector had spotted the trousers strung up outside a known drug dealer's (alleged) door, took this to be a variation on the more usual pair of trainers to signify that supplies had arrived, and moved in to lift anyone in the vicinity who was apparently under twenty-five, mouthy, under the influence of at least one proscribed substance and inappropriately dressed. (I reckon GoPual would have got four out of four there.) Brendy (allegedly) slapped and/or punched an arresting officer; Bree fired off some verbal diarrhoea at said officer and that was that until an ageing hack (Eamonn) was making his duty calls to the police, hospital and fire authority.

Bree was totally sober (surprisingly), clean (not surprisingly) and decently dressed, they reckoned, given the night that was in it. She was in possession of neither an illegal substance, an offensive weapon nor a next-of-kin, despite repeated calls to Sorcha. When Clio arrived *in loco parentis* and told her two of the others were being charged with possession, Bree was filled with sufficient contrition to apologise to he-who-was-given-the-dose-of-the-verbals (who was actually quite hot, she said) and released after caution. No charges, no bail.

'Where are Paul and the rest of them?' Caoimhe asked.

'In the cells. Where they belong. Aimée, I'm starving. I take it Clio baked apple pie? Is there any left? Now,' and she directed this at Darren, with a beaming smile, 'tell me all about your night.'

*

'D'you think Eamonn will put all this in the paper?' Bree whispered as we were dozing off for what remained of the night.

'Undoubtedly,' I said, smiling to myself. Had the girl no concept of libel, *sub judice* etc. etc. etc.?

'Class,' she murmured contentedly. 'I think the Cute Lensman has a good picture of me.'

'Oh, and tell your gran she was *so* right,' she added, digging me in the ribs. 'She's very wise.'

'Where on earth does Gran come into this?'

'The other day, when she was here, I showed her Paul's photo and she warned me off. She said she wouldn't add him to a string of rotten herring to make a dozen.'

The derivation, richness and colour of my progenitor's turn of phrase never ceased to amaze me.

'Of course, all this means I'm single again,' she added contentedly. 'He most definitely was not The One. Better luck next time, Aimée? What do you reckon?'

'Better luck next time, Bree.'

Because Darren is going home in – oh, about fifteen hours. And he'll be asleep for eight of those. And he thinks you're an airhead and he hugged me for two minutes and that's my secret and it's staying that way.

In fact, it could have been three.

Chapter Sixteen

ainbow woke me first. I say 'first' but I mean 'first choice after Clio when he found his breakfast bowl was empty'.

Beside me, Bree lay sleeping the deep sleep of the innocent. I padded to the kitchen to begin the next round of feeding and watering our guests. I heard a subdued murmur from my bedroom so I knocked and shouted through the door.

'Coffee? Juice? I'm feeding Rainbow; do you want anything?'

'I'll pass on the tuna crunchies, thanks, but maybe a slice of toast. I'll give you a hand.' The door opened and out came a fully washed, groomed and dressed Darren Cassidy. And me in my dressing gown, bare feet, no make-up – stop it, Aimée. No more self-flagellation. Wannabe Girl is dead. List-making Girl is history. This is day one of life as Communicator Girl.

'We both woke up and thought we'd best stay awake and get our packing done,' Darren continued, following me into the kitchen. (Thank heavens we had tidied it the night before.) 'Once we've been to Donegal with your dad, it'll be time to head for the coach, more or less.'

'And that's a good thing because I hate lingering good-byes.' This from Caoimhe, who had come and sat on a stool beside us.

'It's flown, Aimée. You know, we were talking about it ourselves. Even if the schools don't go ahead with this programme we want you and your friends to come and stay with us for a weekend. Maybe around New Year? I know Mum and Dad will agree once they see how well this has gone.'

'Yes,' I muttered, 'a mass arrest, two disappearances, a phantom pregnancy scare – it's been such an uneventful two days!'

'Afternoon, people.' Bree made her entrance into the kitchen, still in her gangsta sista outfit from the night before. 'Aimée, let us on to your computer, will you?' she cajoled. 'I just want to get on to Facebook and change my status to single. It's a priority. After all,' she added, as she skipped past, 'I've been single for more than twelve hours.'

'It must be a record,' I whispered to Darren.

'What's that?'

I don't think Bree heard.

'I just said, maybe, as a priority, you'd want to get hold of your mum or find out what's happening to your ex and his mates?'

Bree considered this for all of ten seconds. 'Nah. They're history. I want to disassociate myself from that crowd. Big time.'

'Have you told Paul it's over?' Caoimhe ventured.

'How could I? He wasn't about.'

'Like, he was in the cells?' I suggested.

'Irrelevant. I've got to move on, girls. I'm sure that's what Clio would tell me, Aimée. It's time to reinvent myself. Oh, and I must get in touch with Carly. We need to gossip.'

'What are you going to reinvent yourself as, Bree?' Darren asked innocently, catching my eye.

She shot him a withering look. 'That is such a stupid question. With respect.'

So she hasn't decided yet.

'And what about your mum?' Caoimhe prompted.

'She's out. She'll be fine. She's a big girl now, you know. You worry too much, Caoimhe. Chill.'

The doorbell rang and Bree did us the gracious favour of answering its call.

It was the Da. He walked in and helped himself to coffee with a pained 'don't mind me' expression.

Bree remembered her manners. 'Thanks again for last night, Eamonn. Can I come with you to Donegal, seeing as I am sort of from there? Oh, and let me see what's going to be in the paper tomorrow. About the arrests,' she added unnecessarily.

Eamonn had come prepared and handed her a proof sheet.

'Your mam rang me at work,' he told me. 'They've all been let out now. Brendan and another boy – I think he's a cousin of his; he's another Reilly anyway – they're the only ones who were charged. Disorderly behaviour and assault causing actual bodily harm. They'll be up at the juvenile court next month.'

'Is that it?' Bree held up the proof copy in disbelief. Caoimhe took it and read out loud: 'Two teenagers have been charged with disorderly behaviour and assaulting a police officer near the city centre on Hallowe'en night. The charges arise out of an incident in the Sycamore Heights area. The juveniles, who cannot be identified for legal reasons, are due to appear at the Youth Court in the city next month. At a special hearing of the local Magistrates' Court, a police officer told the court the charges arose out of an incident involving up to thirty young people who had been out celebrating.'

'Boll-*ocks*,' Bree interjected. 'A dozen. Max.'

'It's understood one constable suffered a slight facial injury but did not require hospital treatment. In response to a separate enquiry a police spokesman refused to comment on speculation that they had been acting on a tip-off and that the arrests were part of a covert operation by the Drugs Squad.

'The PSNI spokesman also confirmed that six youths and one female juvenile who were arrested for questioning have been released without charge.'

Bree looked stunned.

'So they didn't even get dope on any of them?'

'I'll pretend I didn't hear that,' Eamonn advised.

'But why aren't all the details there? I can tell you so much more, Eamonn. I'll do an exclusive for you.'

'We couldn't print it, Bree. It's *sub judice*. It's before the court now. We can't use any more than the basic facts as reported in court.'

'So that's all I get? That "one female juvenile" crap?'

The Da tried hard not to smile. 'Afraid so.'

'You wouldn't even know who it was.'

'That's the idea, Bree,' I attempted. 'Anonymity for under-eighteens. Innocent until proven guilty. All that stuff.'

Bree looked crestfallen. 'No pics?'

Eamonn shook his head gravely. 'No pics.'

'Shit. Sorry, Eamonn, but … shit. No one will believe me. Ah well, onwards and upwards. Aimée, your password please …'

Her mobile rang.

'Carly! Wait till you hear what happened …'

'If she wants to come with us, can you get the message to her that she needs to get dressed, quickly?' the Da asked. 'Time's going on. I promised Clio I'd have you all back here for half past four cause she'll be home then to say goodbye. And don't worry,' he whispered to me in the worst stage whisper ever, 'I know you haven't had time this morning so she's getting a few bits and pieces for Darren and Caoimhe to take back to Dublin. I thought we'd take a drive down the coast to Moville and then Fiona's going to meet us for lunch. A late lunch,' he added. 'She's making her own way to join us. I suggested the Bridge Inn. We've got a bit of news to share with you.'

Oh, really?

*

'Does Sorcha know where you are?' Eamonn asked when we eventually prised Bree off my computer and into the back of the car. Through combined effort we had dressed her in a fetching combination of my jeans (leg length skimpy, far too wide) and Caoimhe's sweat-shirt (arm length way too short, width fine) with her gangsta sista platforms. But then the Bridge Inn was never a haven for fashionistas so we were probably OK for dress code.

'Sorcha?' Bree sounded puzzled.

'Yes. Sorcha. Your mother.'

'Maybe I should try her again.' She smiled at this highly original suggestion.

'Mum? Hi! Yes, great, amazing, well, actually, not really but wait till I tell you ...'

It's hard not to eavesdrop in confined spaces, especially with Bree's decibel level. There was much shrieking and ohmyGod-ing bandied to and fro.

''S OK,' Bree reassured us as she rang off. 'Sorcha hasn't been home yet anyway.'

I caught Da's eye in the driver's mirror. I saw Darren looking at Caoimhe.

'I'd better check my texts,' I said to no one in particular as an attempted distraction.

> Tom and I r taking all kids to McDs c u at CG6. Gd to talk, Beksxx njoy 2day.

That told me a lot more than ten minutes' of Bree and Sorcha's mother-daughter interaction. Beks was with Tom, they were with Griffin, Rachael et al, they didn't expect to meet us today but would be there to say goodbye. All must be relatively peaceful, then.

'Oh, shit.' This, unsurprisingly, from Bree. 'I'm out of credit. Go on, Aimée, lend us your phone.'

'Are you ringing Sorcha back?' I handed my phone over to Bree with as much good grace as I could muster.

'No, she's grand. She's busy. I just realised I haven't rung Paul to tell him I'm dumping him. A text would be a bit hard, wouldn't it?'

Bree's ethics are all her own. Incomprehensible but sincere, nonetheless.

*

'Here we are.'

Da had turned off the main cross-border road and pulled up outside what had clearly once been an imposing country house. We all got out of the car and stared at the house. Slates had blown off the roof, the grounds were overgrown and a tree had fallen just beside the front door. Windows were broken or boarded up. The plaster and paintwork were crumbling and flaking. Why, Da, are we here?

'This is a bleak place, isn't it?' Caoimhe spoke for us all and gave a little shudder. 'Why did we stop here? Is it historic or something?'

History, maybe. Please, God, let it have nothing to do with the future. Especially *my* future. Eamonn and Fiona and their 'something to tell me'. They couldn't possibly be thinking of buying this crumbling edifice and converting it into their dream home in the wilds, could they?

Eamonn turned to Darren, all effusive male bonding. 'Let the girls follow us, if they want.' And he steered him away.

We stood, shivered, gazed again at the eerie, hulking ruin and then, by unspoken mutual consent, got back into the car and turned on the heating and the radio, full blast.

*

'Hope we weren't too long.' The Da, getting back into the car, was all artificial bonhomie. Which is not like him. 'I was just telling your brother, Caoimhe,' he went on, feigning spontaneity (badly), 'that Clio would never talk about you behind your back. But she did tell me about how Darren's planning to find out more about his family once he turns eighteen. Clio's very much in favour of finding your roots, all that sort of thing.'

'But you know where you're from!' Bree was surprised.

'I'm not sure.' Darren's tone was unusually reserved.

'What do you mean? Aimée – what is all this about?' This was Bree again. She hates being left out of anything.

'Darren's been telling us that he thinks he may have been adopted, and how nobody will talk to him about it,' I mumbled.

'He doesn't want Mum and Dad to know that he's trying to find things out,' Caoimhe added quickly. 'It'd really upset them.'

'And when Darren told your mum, Aimée, that he'd … em … overheard something that led him to think he might have been born near Derry, Clio asked me to see if I could find this place. Just when we were out for our drive in Donegal.'

'This place being?' Bree was not about to be mollified.

'This was the biggest home for unmarried mothers in the Derry and Raphoe diocese,' Eamonn said.

That explained why it all looked so cheerless. Creepy, even. All those miserable, desperate young girls coming to this awful place in secret.

'Clio knows a fair bit about it,' Eamonn went on. 'Apparently any girls who came looking for help would have stayed here from the time their pregnancy started showing until they went to hospital to have their babies. Then they gave them up for adoption. It's hard to believe this was still going on in your lifetime.'

'Your dad was saying it's a total offchance,' Darren broke in, 'but if it turns out I am adopted, then my birth mum might possibly have stayed here.'

'And what makes you think you're adopted?' Bree wanted answers.

'That's for Darren to tell us when he feels it's right,' said Eamonn. 'Well,' he went on, turning to Darren, all innocence, 'did you get a sense of anything? Any feeling?' This is so not Eamonn's vocabulary. The phrase 'taking the piss' did cross my mind. But if he was, he must have had a reason. Was he trying to shake sense into Darren?

Darren shook his head, paused. Then, 'It's cold,' he said. 'I'm getting hungry. Let's head on.'

It was, as Caoimhe pointed out later, a long way from a four-bedroomed detached in Foxrock with underfloor heating and his own ensuite.

The Da consulted his watch and texted Fiona. At least I assumed it was Fiona. Then we were off along one of the most stunning stretches of coastline in Europe, towards Moville.

Keep calm, I counselled myself. Communication Girl, right? Just *ask*. Ask your father about the big announcement. Then you can prepare yourself mentally. And facially. Rehearse the required response.

It had to be a baby. Mrs O'Hara, the hospital, the hints … But why in front of Bree and the Cassidys? And when Clio's not here? Does she already know? She is so used to keeping confidences; I'd never know. But she would hint, wouldn't she? No, probably not.

And why should it matter to me?

'Turn left! Now! Up here – please,' shrieked Bree, shattering the ambience. 'Eamonn, up here and down this lane then first right.'

'We're not near the Bridge Inn yet –'

'Noo! Not the pub. This is the way to Willie's.'

'You didn't say you wanted to call on him,' Eamonn said.

'Well, I didn't know I was going to call in because I didn't know we would be going near his farm, did I? I only just realised it myself, Eamonn, so don't be embarrassed. I mean, one tree and one field looks much like another doesn't it? But I know I'm right. Yes, that house there.'

We pulled up in the yard of a small stone farmhouse. A tall, angular man in a navy boiler suit with a weather-beaten face and hands leaned against a fence post. He watched as a slender figure in oversized jeans and an undersized sweatshirt teetered round the piles of cow dung to embrace him.

Darren turned his head.

'Willie,' I explained lamely. 'Bree's dad.'

'*He's* Bree's dad?'

Eamonn and I nodded in unison. It seemed such an anomaly of nature.

*

'I just gave Willie a brief outline of what happened last night,' Bree assured us as we walked into the bar. 'It's better that way. I felt I had to, in case he sees it in the paper.'

Unless you cut it out and show it to him, I thought, he isn't going to see it in the paper.

'He's happier in his innocence. Trust me. And,' Bree beamed expansively, 'lunch is on me. No, Eamonn, you have been more than good running us about. This is my treat. Well, Willie's treat. He insisted.'

She pressed a bundle of well-thumbed twenty Euro notes into my da's hand.

His gaze was fixed on the figure seated with a drink in the corner of the lounge. Fiona. We went to join her. Darren pulled together two tables and the waiter passed round laminated menus while recommending the roast of the day.

'Everything else will be microwaved,' Fiona counselled. 'I'd go for that.'

By common assent we ordered six plates of turkey and ham and waited while they were placed in front of us; huge helpings on scalding hot plates which fairly bounced when the potatoes (roast and creamed), carrots and peas were added in agricultural portions.

'Just veg for me,' Bree smiled at the waiter. 'I'm lacto-ovo-vegetarian.'

'Since when?' I spluttered.

'Since I became single.'

'Best not have any gravy then, just in case.' Darren sweetly removed the stainless steel boat from her hand. 'And there's probably gelatine in the trifle. Cows' hooves, you know.'

Bree nodded sadly. She loved trifle.

The atmosphere was more relaxed than I expected (go, Communication Girl!), partly because we were all starving and shovelling down massive portions at record speed and you can't be stand-offish with a faceful of mash, peas and gravy. Darren and Caoimhe were generous in their praise of all things Derry/McCourt-Logan. Bree treated Fiona to The Arrest, Version Three.

Fiona told us she knew a bit about the history of the home we'd seen. It had definitely been closed since the millennium, she said. All the files for the children born there would be with the public records office in the relevant centre – Dublin or Belfast – and the building was now for sale as it was surplus to requirements. But, she added, it was in such a dilapidated condition that, given the state of the housing market, it would be nigh on impossible to sell.

'It's such a coincidence,' she added. 'When Eamonn said where he was taking you today, I gave off to him and said that's the place I've been telling you about this past month and trying to get you to go and look at.'

For one surreal moment I thought my nightmare scenario was indeed coming true. She was going to say the Da and she were going to buy it as the family seat for a dynasty – as yet, perhaps, unborn. (She was drinking mineral water but then she *was* driving.)

Words hung in the air round me and I fixed a silly half-smile on my face until a single phrase filtered through.

'And that's why I'll be away until Christmas,' she was explaining.

Eh?

'The Trust want me to spend at least six weeks observing in their state of the art prototype,' she went on, 'although I'd really like a lot longer. Just to get a better insight into what we're planning for here. It'll be cross-border and cross-community,' she explained, sounding like Clio. 'And it'll be the first of its kind in the north-west – in Ireland, actually. We're looking at next April. I'm sorry, Aimée, I'm boring you,' she finished with a smile.

April. Well outside any gestation period.

'Not at all.' I smiled back and silently entreated the assembled company for a lifeline. Any lifeline. *What* had she just said?

'I think it's a brilliant idea,' Bree was saying. 'And if people like Mrs O'Hara think it's a great idea – well, she's an expert.'

'She's an amazing woman,' Fiona agreed. 'So she told you she'd met me a few times while she was at the ante-natal clinic? That's where I did most of my research.'

'She has an amazing eldest daughter,' I said.

'Exactly,' Fiona went on intensely. 'But how many new mothers don't have that support? That's why we had the idea of establishing a cross-border Trust where new mums – any mums, but maybe first-time mums and those with little or no support, in particular – could come for a day or a residential to meet up and to learn practical parenting skills in a safe and confidential environment. To build up their confidence and set up a support network to call on.'

Did the Da realise how like the Mammy Fiona sounded? Mammy in counselling mode, that is.

'Your mother's department has been very positive about the whole idea,' Fiona went on, 'and no doubt Eamonn will give us a two-page spread when it's at advanced planning stage. But it's embargoed until the sale is agreed.'

I looked at Bree, who clearly had no comprehension of what this meant. I'd kill her later.

'So, I'll be away from Friday until just before Christmas,' Fiona went on, 'and I'm relying on you to help get your dad organised for the festive season.'

This was trying to be nice, generational outreach, whatever you wanted to call it, on a grand scale. It would have been mean not to meet her halfway. After all, it's hardly my fault that I have two parents who are incapable of living with each other and, very possibly, with anyone else.

I fear it may be hereditary.

'Fiona.'

Darren touched her arm.

'You know what you said about the records.'

'Yes?'

'Well, if anyone thought they had been adopted, how could they go about accessing them? Once they turned eighteen, like?'

Beside me, Caoimhe groaned and whispered, 'Leave it.'

But Fiona was already in full professional voice, explaining to Darren how any hypothetical person would go about tracing his lineage. Both of them knew exactly who the hypothetical person was, of course.

Mercifully, this prompted Bree to elaborate to Caoimhe on her own genealogy. At some length and with added colour. From the corner of my eye, I saw the brown envelope being taken from the back pocket of Darren's jeans. Then I saw Fiona huddle closer to the Da and Darren. There was some urgent whispering but, strain as I might, I couldn't hear. Damn.

*

'So you knew all about Fiona and the big Health Trust thing?' I accused Clio later, while we were hanging about at the school, waiting for the coach to load.

'The parenting centre? Yes, but it's embargoed. That reminds me, I'll speak to Bree about Sorcha. I think she's lost interest by now, though.'

Clio looked across the pitch to where Bree was holding court to a captive audience of Year 9s about her prison experience. There were quite a few Year 11 and 12 lads hanging round, too, obviously attracted by the loud and frequent use of the phrase 'newly single'. Not to mention the strange garb.

'Were you really worrying Fiona and Eamonn were pregnant?' Clio squeezed my shoulders. 'You are a strange wee thing at times, Aimée. Or maybe not. Would you have minded?'

'Would you?' I threw back the question.

'I'd be delighted for them. But only when, and if, the time is right for them. And if Fiona wants to see this scheme through, that'll not be for a couple of years yet. She's a very bright woman,' Clio said without any trace of irony.

I had to remind myself of one of Gran's more acerbic yet insightful observations about her daughter: 'Clio comes across as so accepting and so PC about herself and Eamonn. What most people don't realise is that underneath that philanthropic exterior lurks the soul of a woman who thinks that, on balance, the praying mantis gets it right.'

Rebekah came over to join us.

'I'm going up to the hospital after this,' she explained. 'For visiting time. I've never met Tom's mum before. Physically, she's well on the way to recovery. She'll be home by the weekend and he wants to move back there as soon as possible. So does Griffin.'

'Maybe this time ...'

'Maybe nothing, Aimée.'

Rebekah was so sensible. So mature. Accepting? I don't know. Very fond of Tom? Yes. I knew when to shut up.

'Thank you so much for the gifts,' Caoimhe said. 'We haven't decided yet what to keep for ourselves and what to give Mum and Dad.' She hugged us in turn. 'I'm just waiting for Darren now. Can you believe the big pseud is signing autographs?'

'Sadly, yes,' I conceded. 'There's not much excitement round Castle Grove.'

Then we thought about what I'd just said. And we started to laugh and laugh.

And I only had time to hug Caoimhe and help her on board and hug Darren for slightly longer than was necessary before Mizz was snapping at my heels like a Tasmanian devil and jabbing at her watch.

'I'll ring you tonight,' Darren whispered. 'I couldn't get you on your own and I owe it to Caoimhe to talk to her first. I have a bit of news.'

Oh?

'Now,' he went on, loudly (to my delight), 'be sure and keep in touch, won't you, Aimée? And I'm going to set up my own email account and stop using Caoimhe's. I was never motivated enough. Before.'

Before the twinning?

Before Castle Grove?

Before Derry?

Before – me? Me, Aimée Logan?

Too much.

Thank goodness it was time to go.

Caoimhe, Darren and me – we don't do prolonged goodbyes.

*

'It was … interesting.'

That was Clio's opening gambit as she folded the second load of washing. The airbed was as deflated as I was and the camp bed was back in its box awaiting collection. Yellow Post-its listed groceries to be replaced, calls to be made, paperwork to be processed. Normality.

'It was.' I was proceeding with caution.

'Caoimhe's a lovely girl. Very appreciative. And I think Darren may be a bit happier now. I've told him I really think he should open up to his parents but it's up to him.'

Darren and Clio? A private counselling session?

'I know he showed you his birth certificate,' Clio went on, nonchalantly. 'He showed it to me, too.'

'And my da and Fiona. In the pub.'

Clio was unfazed.

'I'd mentioned it to Fiona – in confidence, of course. I just wanted to double check something, though I was ninety nine per cent sure I was right.'

Our eyes met.

'Maybe let Darren tell you?'

'Maybe you should prepare me?'

'Maybe I should teach you a bit more about birth certificates? Hypothetically?'

'Maybe you should, Mammy. It might be useful.'

'Even though we established during that … unsettled
… phase of yours, when you were nine, that you're most
definitely not adopted. And you know that both
Eamonn and I believe adopted children should be
brought up knowing that they are. From day one.
Honesty and accountability.'

'Yes, Mammy.'

'And that you should be able to talk to your parents
about anything. Well, nearly anything.'

'Mm-hm.'

'In an ideal world.'

'Of course.'

'Well …'

We come together holding our opposite corners of the
sheet to fold it for storage.

'I think it's a safe bet that Darren is the genetic offspring of Patrick Joseph Cassidy and Susan Anne Cassidy,
née Kealey.'

'Like it says on his birth certificate.'

Clio nodded. 'Yes. Except she may not have been
Susan Cassidy then. Not that marriage is in any way relevant to good parenting –'

I stopped the impending lecture. 'But surely you have
to register a child within a month of its birth or something? Not four years?'

'OK. Point taken. But there's no big mystery. I was
fairly sure straight away. I had to try not to smile.' Clio

smiled then, conspiratorially. 'Fiona came to exactly the same conclusion. We've seen dozens of certificate copies like that. Both of us.'

She sat down on the bed.

'When a baby's born, both parents' names go on the birth certificate. Obviously. Unless, for whatever reason, the child's registered as 'father unknown'. Now, it's true that adopted children don't get access to their birth mother's details until they are adults themselves.'

'Eighteen.'

'Yes. But if the parents aren't married at the time of birth and subsequently do get married, they can apply to have a copy of the birth certificate issued in the mother's married name.'

'Go on.' I could feel another impending lecture on the folly of changing one's surname. And I wanted Clio to get to the point.

'But a lot don't bother,' Clio continued. 'They just assume the birth has been, to use an old fashioned word, "legitimised" by the marriage. It's only when the child is about to start school that they realise they need to apply for a copy which obscures the disparity. All for the sake of keeping up appearances –'

'Mammy!'

'OK. But I am confident – and so is Fiona – that when Darren either turns eighteen or finds the courage to approach his parents in a civilised and non-con-frontational manner, whichever comes first, he will get the confirmation that they married some time between his birth in March 1995 and Caoimhe's arrival in December 1996. I'd guess the summer of 1995, if I was a betting woman.

'His mum would have been about thirty-six or thirty-seven and his dad would have been in his forties when they discovered Darren was on the way. Sooner than expected.' She grinned. 'They could hardly say they were young and naïve. And they would have seen themselves as fine upstanding Catholics. I think it must have been embarrassing for them – at least, that's the way I put it to Darren when he discussed it with me. Hypothetically, of course. It helped him feel less embarrassed about his own naïvety,' she added with a smile.

So Clio and Darren had discussed this. Darren and Fiona? Fiona and Clio? Fiona and Eamonn? Clio and Eamonn?

Why was I the last to know?

Or could the answer be that it was none of my business? And it was, after all, hypothetical.

I was almost stuck for words. But not quite.

'If that's what happened, it would explain why they're overprotective,' I said. 'They're probably scared of history repeating itself. Not that it should matter,' I added quickly. I have to think of Clio's feelings, you know. Single parents can be uber-sensitive about their status.

She nodded. 'And it would explain Mrs Cassidy's overreaction when Darren asked to see his original birth certificate. And he put two and two together and made ten. Typical.'

Thus, as I have observed before, do rumours start. And speculation. And worry. Until fiction becomes accepted fact. Castle Grove is right. So is Clio. Openness and accountability.

'But let him tell you himself,' Clio advised, 'and he will. After he stops feeling silly. And embarrassed – not at his parents, but at his own carry-on. It's the twenty-first century, for heaven's sake. And after he tells Caoimhe. I hope he tells her, soon. It'll be a weight off her mind, I should think. She's such a caring wee girl. Men!'

We smiled.

'I think the sight of that sad, sad place, that mother and baby home, brought him down to earth,' Clio added wryly. 'It might have made him think Foxrock has its good points.'

'I'll put the kettle on.'

She was going out the door when the thought struck me.

'Mammy, what about this thing he talks about, how his parents brought him from Derry?'

'I reckon he'll find that it wasn't Derry. It was Kerry. That's where Mrs Cassidy's from, originally. I knew she wasn't a Dub the minute I spoke to her on the phone. I mentioned it when we were making small talk. And she told me she's a native Kerrywoman. "Born, bred and buttered" was the phrase. That's the danger of eavesdropping and of half-hearing things and making assumptions,' Mam observed, her eyes twinkling. 'You can go off at completely the wrong tangent. Not that *you'd* ever do it, Aimée,' she added.

'Of course not,' I agreed, tongue very firmly in cheek. 'Mammy?'

'What, love?'

'Do you think, if Darren knew all this, and he was happy that he was a hundred per cent Cassidy, and he had no connections with Derry whatsoever, he would still have blagged a place on the exchange trip?'

'Oh, undoubtedly.' She shrugged her shoulders. 'Why wouldn't he? Free access to a bevy of girls? And the European capital of Hallowe'en? He's a bloke, isn't he?'

Yes, mother, he is. He definitely is. I can vouch for that.

From: caoimheimneverwrong@mail.net
To: aimeemcclogan@derry.com
22.20

Hi Aimée,
I can't believe it's all over for now! It was truly the best experience of my school life. Maybe even my life so far. One crazy thing after another. Please thank Clio and Eamonn once again for all their kindness and tell them Mum loved the brooch and Dad was chuffed with the books. They're going to write, too.

Thank your friends for all the CRAIC! I'll be on Facebook tomorrow!

I hope I can convince Mum and Dad to let me stand on my own two feet a bit more (no pun intended) and Darren and I are already planning when you may come and visit us.

Love to Clio and Eamonn and Beks and Tom and Bree and Rainbow from your best virtual friend,

Caoimhe.

PS Already Mum says she sees Darren more
'settled', as she puts it, and asks what
happened 'up North'?! Even I can't
answer that!!

PPS He wants to talk to me later - do
you know about this? X

Mercifully, this no longer needed answering as I saw
another email from Caoimhe in my inbox.

Stand by the computer!! I've told the
big bro - DEFINITELY the big bro - to
mail you asap. Otherwise I'll tell you
myself. Maybe now he will learn to take
himself a bit less seriously! It's our
secret for now, till he decides to raise
it with The Parents.

Caoimhe

From darrenr8sderry@mail.net
To: aimeemcclogan@derry.com
00.17

Hi Aimée,
I had a chat with Caoimhe tonight and I
know, because Clio promised me, she will
have had a chat with you about the same
thing. The Big Mystery that isn't. (Cringe
or what?) Nothing definite, of course, but
it seems there was a slight embarrassment
over the timeline for my conception, birth
and my parents' marriage. It's weird to

think that mattered a generation ago but
then it'd probably still matter to them
today ... I was what your Granny might
well call 'a wee surprise' and, as Clio
reminded me, unplanned doesn't mean
unwanted. I'm not going to say anything to
Mum and Dad for now. I can't see who would
benefit from it. Hopefully they'll never
know I know. (Sort of.) That way they'll
never know how close I came to making a
total prat of myself.

(Please tell me I didn't ...)

I keep thinking about that place,
though. Women just must have been in
despair to go there. It was scary.

Derry was great. Really amazing. Thanks
for everything and also to your folks,
including Rainbow. Please pass on my
address to Tom as I'd love to keep in
touch. And remember me to the girls! I
will definitely be back when I'm
eighteen, for my interview at Magee
(there's confidence!) but hopefully long
before then, too.

Meantime, Aimée, if you can cope with a
100% Dub who really, really doesn't do
Facebook, can we be Facebook friends?

Darren x

Felicity McCall

From: aimeemcclogan@derry.com
To: caoimheimneverwrong@mail.net
3:30

Night Caoimhe x.
I hope it works out.
See you soon.

From: aimeemcclogan@derry.com
To: Darrenr8sderry@mail.net
3:35

Night, Darren

I thought you'd never ask.

Aimée
Xox